THE STUPENDOUS ADVENTURES OF MIGHTY MARTY HAYES

THE STUPENDOUS ADVENTURES OF MIGHTY MARTY HAYES

LORA L. HYLER

HenschelHAUS Publishing, Inc.
Milwaukee, Wisconsin

Quantity discounts are available for schools and other groups. Please contact HenschelHAUS Publishing, Inc. for information.

Published by
HenschelHAUS Publishing, Inc.
www.henschelHAUSbooks.com

ISBN: 978159598-588-0
E-ISBN: 978159598-589-1
Audio ISBN: 978159598-599-6
LCCN: 2017964751

Cover design by: Ian Wade, St. Philip, Barbados
Instagram.com/dracanimaart/

I dedicate this work to my family and extended family, the village, readers of children's books everywhere and all who are on the journey toward publication.

And to my kindred spirits who have a passion: follow that passion, wherever it leads. The thing that excites you, did not come to you by chance. Realize you must put in the work. It's all in the preparation and I promise you, you will reap the rewards.

1
MARTY'S FIRST DAY
OF 7TH GRADE

O n the first day, and first hour of 7th grade, Marty Hayes walked down the hallway toward the Advanced Science 303 classroom of Windsor Middle School with Christopher Chadwick, his best friend since kindergarten. He knew they would spend the first semester of class working with the new CRISPR-Cas9 gene editing technique, and Marty couldn't have been more excited.

Worldwide, the Zika virus was big news. He wasn't surprised when he saw a full page spread in one of his mom's travel magazines. But, it was a small story on the same page that captured his interest. All summer, he had read every article he could get his hands on about CRISPR-Cas9.

"So, genes can be spliced to prevent disease in the human body?" Christopher asked.

"That's right. But, that's not what we'll work on this semester," Marty said, adjusting his backpack. "I read in the article that maybe one day the genome of mosquitoes could be re-engineered so they can't reproduce, leading to extinction. That's what we'll be working hands on with...mosquitoes."

They entered the classroom, jostling each other and sizing up the colorful posters of frog autopsies, biographies of Marie Curie, and Neil deGrasse Tyson. They noted the array of colorful beakers, tongs, test tubes, microscopes, Bunsen Burners. The science classroom staple: a visual of the periodic table of elements was prominently displayed.

Marty and Christopher shared a love of the outdoors, and all things science and spy-related. The International Spy Museum in Washington, D.C. was a favorite hangout of theirs. In person, they had visited only once. Birthday money, cash from weekly allowances and small chores had netted them each a hefty arsenal of spy gear.

Marty's chubby brown face, sharp nose, and round glasses, revealed Einstein-like concentration. His buddy Christopher ran his fingers through his mop of blondish-brown hair and wrinkled his freckled nose. Marty knew that was a sign

Christopher couldn't wait to get started with whatever Mr. Bunsen had in store for them.

Their new science teacher had a reputation of getting right to work on the first day of class. No boring syllabus and reciting classroom rules for him.

Marty turned his attention to the white board at the front. Mr. Bunsen wiped his bald head, and with his right hand, wrote his name in large, rounded letters.

"Good morning, class. I'm Mr. Bunsen," he said.

Snickers rippled throughout the room. Marty and Christopher exchanged glances.

"Yes, like the Bunsen burner. I've heard all the jokes, so spare me. That's if you know what's good for you," he added, ominously peering at the class over his horn-rimmed specs. He adjusted his too tight suspenders, creating new wrinkles in his button down plaid shirt.

"Rather than waste time with all the preliminaries, I'd like to demonstrate why, if it isn't already, science will become your favorite subject. First, I need to divide you up into groups of three or four."

Marty began to bounce in his seat with excitement. He was disappointed when he and

Christopher wound up in separate groups. Then, he noticed his group included a cute, curly-haired girl with honey-colored skin and bright, pink lips. She was dressed all in royal purple.

"Wow!" Marty said under his breath. "My lucky day!"

Mr. Bunsen was now standing directly over him holding a large tray of Petri dishes. "Did everyone get that?" he asked pointedly, gazing down. Marty quickly nodded, figuring his group could catch him up later. Mr. Bunsen carefully set a Petri dish filled with some withered substance in front of Marty's group and moved on.

"What's this all about?" Marty asked, peering at the label.

"Guess we better get to these instructions," a boy responded. Marty vaguely remembered him from last year. He waved a sheet under Marty's nose.

Marty caught Christopher's eye at the next table and gave a slight nod to his left. Christopher followed his buddy's gaze and feasted his eyes for the next couple of minutes on the vision of loveliness on his best friend's team. Marty grinned widely. Then he noticed Wade, the school's top bully, next to Christopher.

"Sorry, old buddy, Christopher. Not your day," Marty muttered under his breath.

He ignored the disappointed sounds of classmates expecting an easy first day. Marty examined the instructions at hand, eager to see what his new science teacher had in store for them.

"Wow! I can't believe we're going to work with mosquitoes and the CRISPR-Cas9 kit on the first day of class!"

"Oh, I need a volunteer to distribute the beakers," Mr. Bunsen said nodding to a counter in the far corner of the room. Wade's arm shot up.

Mr. Bunsen nodded. Out of the corner of his eye, Marty noticed Mr. Bunsen heading for the door. Must be getting more Petri dishes, Marty thought. Wade grabbed his team's paper.

"I'm the team leader," Wade said. "Everyone knows in science, I'm the best in the whole school. We're working with Clustered Regularly Inter-Spaced Palindromic Repeats. If you don't know about this, you're in the wrong classroom. No room for you in Advanced Science 303."

Marty glanced at Wade, who had terrorized his younger classmates since kindergarten. He looked like he had grown a whole foot over the summer. His mousy brown hair was unusually long and unruly. After so many years, Christopher and Marty had reached a truce of sorts with him. They minded their own business and he agreed to stay away from their friends. Most of the time, anyway.

Mr. Bunsen hadn't been properly introduced to Wade. Who could blame him for picking the first hour of the first class of the new school year to duck out of the classroom for a minute or two?

Marty saw Wade fling his group's instructions to Christopher.

"You're the reader. I'm the chemist," Wade said.

Christopher shrugged. Their third team member was a rail thin, quiet bespectacled boy with buck teeth, who Marty didn't recognize.

"I'm Tim. What can I do?"

"Clean up," Wade barked, causing the tiny Tim to nearly fall out of his chair.

Marty shook his head and turned back to the instructions. "Don't worry about the long name for the CRISPR-Cas9," he told his group. "All you really need to know is that scientists all over the world are excited about this. And we're the lucky 7th graders who get to target and modify DNA."

Marty's team nodded.

Christopher began reading. Tim sat mute. Marty saw Wade hop up, and grab a glass container from his backpack. He then dashed over, and hovered over the tray of beakers.

Just as he thought of investigating, the cute girl asked Marty, "When are we going to start? The instructions say we'll work with mosquitoes all semester long, and today's experiment is worth 10 points."

Marty noticed Wade's flushed face as he skipped around the room, adding an unknown ingredient to the Petri dishes of his classmates. If they hadn't had a personal encounter, most would have heard of Wade's reputation by now. No one dared challenge him. Wade returned several minutes later to his team, giggling, flushing bright red. Fear? No. Excitement? Hmm.

Marty shook his head wondering when Wade became so helpful. Just as the thought crossed his mind, he heard a low buzz. But, he was distracted by a bright citrusy scent that could only be coming from—the lovely girl donned all in purple.

"What's your name?" Marty asked.

"Eye-ee-sha. Only, it's spelled with an A. Aisha," she said slowly.

"Aisha, I'm Marty. Short for Martin, like Dr. Martin Luther King, Jr. and my grandad."

"And I'm Johnny," the third kid said. "Whatever you do, don't call me John."

"Got it. Well, it looks like we've got an insect experiment," Marty touched each ingredient in turn. "Beaker filled with some liquid that we need to inject. Mini bottle of some other liquid. Petri dish full of toasted mosquitoes. Science tongs. Eye dropper. Microscope. Containment device. Cool."

He studied the instructions. "So, according to the sheet, it's all here. Who wants to read, who wants to mix, and who wants to play with bugs?"

Marty's team quickly agreed on roles, each donning a pair of the safety glasses that lay on their table. The cute girl deftly grabbed the large beaker, and peered into the Petri dish. Its smoky charcoal color masked whatever was going on inside.

"Something is moving around in there. I can't quite make it out," Aisha said.

"Be careful with that until we figure out what we're working with," Marty said.

Aisha nodded, never taking her eyes off her work. Marty allowed himself a satisfied grin with his new classmate. She appeared to be just as fascinated with the first day science experiment as he was.

Mr. Bunsen re-entered the classroom. "How's it going? Any questions? Not too many teachers would give you a real live experiment on the first day, am I right?" He seemed very pleased with himself. Marty saw Tim raise his hand. The look Wade shot him stopped him in his tracks. Tim began coughing loudly.

"Now, remember, keep on the safety glasses. At the count of three, I want your designated team member to carefully take your Petri dish and using your dropper, place a couple of drops in. Are we ready? 3, 2, 1..."

Marty heard it before he saw the frantic buzzing of excited mosquitoes. As kids ducked under desks and ran aimlessly around the room, swarming mosquitoes began to infiltrate room 217. Marty's eyes darted back and forth between his cowering classmates, as the insects began to find targets and identify feeding spots. Chairs toppled and kids darted here and there to escape the ferociously biting insects. Wade clapped his hands and giggled.

Marty glanced at Mr. Bunsen rooted to his spot just inside the classroom door, watching in horror at his glorious first day experiment gone wrong. Marty knew that feeling. As he realized he had powers to create and bring to life things he imagined, he had freaked out a little. Especially, when it would take a while to rein in a creation.

Buzzing mosquitoes were everywhere. Marty wondered what had sent them into such a frenzied state. The smell of fear was overtaking the class-room.

With all the commotion, Marty glimpsed at, but didn't quite register a large silver and black drone hovering just outside the classroom window. Its yellow and green flickering lights were recording every action happening inside the science classroom.

Suddenly, he sprung into action. He lifted his shirt displaying a belt loaded with spy gear, grabbed an ultrasonic whistle and blew. Wade laughed hysterically. Time slowed. Marty blew with one hand and grabbed his team's Petri dish with the other. He tensed his face in a study of fierce concen-tration. With the rest of the class, he watched as the mosquitoes heeded a call that didn't register with humans. The frantic insects flew in groups to the dish.

With his wide-eyed classmates in awe, Marty calmly deposited the dying hoard into the trash. Mr. Bunsen managed to move his feet and shift his body forward.

"Ah," was the only sound Marty heard in the classroom as the once fierce mosquitoes fell silent. The sound of buzzing was replaced with twenty kids scratching. Mr. Bunsen reached for a welt forming on his forehead.

Wade smiled smugly. "Can we do another CRISPR-Cas9 experiment, Mr. Bunsen?"

"My first day science experiment. Ruined," Mr. Bunsen responded.

* * * * *

Minutes later, Marty and Christopher sat at a lunch table reliving the incident.

"It was just my luck getting stuck with old Wade and you get the prettiest girl in the whole school on your team," Christopher moaned.

"Yeah," Marty agreed, lost in the memory of first setting eyes on her. There were lots of pretty girls at Windsor, but there was something special about this one. She was pretty without seeming to be self-conscious about it. And she was smart. He noticed she didn't hesitate to dive into a science experiment on the first day of school.

"Did you even get her name?" Christopher asked, biting into a thick turkey sandwich. Mayonnaise oozed down his chin.

"Of course, I did. Aisha. She just moved here this summer. From L.A." Marty grabbed another potato chip, leaving his tuna sandwich untouched.

"How did you get that information?" Christopher screamed, spewing mayo in all directions.

"Hey! Would you keep your germs to yourself?" Marty yelled, "You're getting mayo on my chips! We've had one disaster too many already today." He leaned back in his chair and munched thoughtfully on a chip.

"And to answer your question, I have my ways, my man. I have my ways."

2
MR. BUNSEN: 0
GRANNY: 1

Mr. Bunsen got out of his car, and looked around the subdivision marked by patches of mature trees, colorful flowers, groomed lawns and attractive ranch homes. From his bedroom window, Marty watched as his science teacher double-checked his phone, nodded, and quickened his stride toward the front door. Marty spotted a model-sized Lamborghini whiz into view.

Mr. Bunsen had to climb over a small collection of wires and gear strewn across the front lawn. Spy stuff. He walked around the bright pink girl's bicycle with racing stripes and red, yellow and pink streamers shooting out of each handlebar.

Toni was busy today. Marty worried whether she had gotten into his spy gear again. He slowly crept down the stairs and positioned himself on the landing where he could clearly see the front door and hear any living room conversation without anyone knowing. Time tested and verified.

Suddenly, the front door swung open.

"Oh, hello there," Mr. Bunsen stammered. "I was just about to knock."

"Yes?"

Marty smiled at the sight of his beloved granny, all five feet of her looking up at his science teacher, who had to be six feet tall or more. Her stance was erect and proud as she peered over her eyeglasses at the stranger. Her wiry, gray hair stood on her head, each strand standing at opposing angles.

"Are you Mrs. Hayes?" he asked. "I'm Mr. Bunsen, Marty's science teacher."

Granny extended her hand. "I'm Mrs. Michaels, Marty's granny. Everyone calls me that."

"Oh, happy to meet you, Mrs.…. Granny. Mind if I come in?"

"No use standing on the front porch," she said with a wink, stepping aside. "I know how my grandson loves science, so anybody following in the steps of Madam Curie and Albert Einstein is more than welcome in this home!"

At that, Marty could have sworn Mr. Bunsen puffed out his chest a bit. Within minutes, they were enjoying a cup of coffee.

"I hope you like it," said Granny.

"Oh, this is very delicious. Coconut Hazelnut?"

"I like a man who knows his coffee."

Marty took in the buttery smell from where he sat. Though he didn't like the taste of coffee, Marty thought he could join Granny sometime. That's if he could add a few spoonfuls of sugar and chocolate. He saw his teacher looking around at the spotless living room. Marty involuntarily ducked, making sure Mr. Bunsen didn't spot him from his perch on the staircase.

A flurry of activity began quickly moving toward Granny and Mr. Bunsen, who jumped at the sight. When the tornado stopped, Marty spotted Toni. He had once overheard his mom's friend describe his baby sister as an "adorable, brown-skinned girl with large, inquisitive eyes, lovely pigtails, and amazing curiosity." He would describe her as trouble. Her bright pink outfit was topped with an over-sized man's tie. Marty saw Mr. Bunsen's double take. Toni ran up to Granny and made clicking movements using the tie, then peered at Mr. Bunsen's face and did the same.

"Toni, stop that!" Granny yelled. She turned to Mr. Bunsen, "I'm sorry. This is Toni, Marty's little sister and my granddaughter. She's gotten into Marty's camera tie again." She pulled the little girl close. "And from the looks of it, she's been in his fingerprint powder again, too."

Marty had to put his hands over his mouth to keep from yelling out at Toni. "How many times have I asked her to stay out of my stuff?" he muttered to himself.

"Camera tie? Fingerprint powder?" Mr. Bunsen asked, leaning in with interest.

"Yes, and the last time her mom found out about her meddling in Marty's things, she couldn't have a play date for a month. Remember, Toni?" she asked, pointedly.

Toni nodded vigorously, her pigtails bouncing. "Granny, don't tell. I'll put it back." Granny smiled and watched the youngster leave the room.

"So the kids like spy stuff?" Mr. Bunsen asked.

"Like? Now that's the understatement of the century. These children would spend every penny they get on spy stuff, if they could. It's a harmless hobby," she quickly added. "So, what brings you here, Mr. Bunsen?"

"Oh, yes. I'm here about Marty," he said, taking a gulp of his coffee.

Marty leaned in a bit.

"He's not in trouble already, is he?" Granny asked. Marty heard the concern in her voice.

"No. In fact, I'd have to say he saved the day," Mr. Bunsen said with a chuckle. "You see, I decided to have a little fun with my science classes on the first day of school. Over the summer, I acquired a CRISPR-Cas9 kit."

"A what kind of kit?" Granny asked.

"Oh, it's a great development in the world of science. Scientists have developed a novel way to alter DNA. I purchased a kit so my classes can work with mosquitoes to render the female incapable of reproducing. With this advanced class of students, I thought it would be great to get them in on some real research with such potential."

"I'm following you so far," said Granny.

"Everything was going along just fine until the eggs hatched and somehow became mosquitoes, that then got out and attacked the kids..."

"Attacked the kids?" Granny interrupted.

"Well, y-y-yes. You see, without my knowledge, someone or some groups added a batch of live mosquitoes. These mosquitoes were overstimulated. I left the room for just a moment..." he hurriedly explained. "When I returned, things were quite out of control..."

"The kids are all right?" Granny asked, leaning forward.

"Yes. I was able to test one of the captured mosquitoes. Even though, for the life of me..."

Marty smiled. Granny was using her 'what the heck were you thinking?' voice. How would Mr. Bunsen get out of this?

"I'm embarrassed to say it wasn't me who snagged the mosquitoes. It was, well, Marty. That's why I'm here. I've never seen anything quite like it..."

"What do you mean?" Granny asked in the tone she used when she scolded Marty or Toni for doing something she had told them not to do. Mr. Bunsen fidgeted in his seat.

"Well, he somehow managed to coax the mos-quitoes from all of the students' dishes back into a single Petri dish. It's as if he willed them to return. How he could have reacted that quickly...It stopped everything in its tracks," Mr. Bunsen finished, and scratched his head.

Granny met Marty's science teacher's words with silence, and then cleared her throat. "Mr. Bunsen, what you just described to me is some sort of miracle. It was quite heroic of my grandson to do what he did. I mean, after you so foolishly set up such a dangerous experiment, only to leave the room..."

Marty smiled as Mr. Bunsen shifted uncomfortably. "I'm really sorry about that. I stepped out for only a couple of minutes, and yes, I appreciate what Marty did. The reason I'm here is I've been trying to recreate what happened, and for the life of me, I can't figure out how a 7th grader was able to tame swarming mosquitoes. I've never seen insects so ferocious. They went into total submission. They were so spent, they died on the spot. It was quite extraordinary, you see."

"What are you saying?" Granny asked. Again, Marty recognized the annoyance in her voice.

"Why, I'm just wondering...This DNA research has great possibilities..." Mr. Bunsen's voice trailed off as Granny stared at him. Her eyes are likely changing color, Marty thought, in the way they do when she's angry.

"Mr. Bunsen, as I see it, you created a little experiment and left the children in your charge unattended. My grandson's quick thinking not only saved the day, but likely saved the classroom...and your job," Granny said and sat back in her chair.

"Yes, ma'am. I think you've made yourself quite clear," said Mr. Bunsen, setting down his cup of coffee with shaking hands. "Thank you. And I'll see myself out."

Marty watched as Mr. Bunsen abruptly stood up and made his way to the front door. Granny, close on his heels, gave him a quick wave and closed the door soundly behind him. Marty bounded down the stairs.

"Was that my science teacher?" he asked, attempting innocence.

"I guess you can call him that," Granny said huffily. "I'm not sure what kind of teacher runs a science experiment that leaves students alone to serve as insect bait." She continued muttering under her breath as she walked away.

Marty flung open the door. As he stepped outside, he looked down to see Toni's frowning face, carefully testing the fingerprints on the door knob, using a kit of some kind.

"Oh, don't worry, I'm sure they're fine. I'll just send these to the lab," she said with an angelic first grader's smile, gazing up at Mr. Bunsen, who stood on the front steps.

"How are you, Mr. Bunsen?" Marty asked.

"Oh, hi, Marty. I was just having a chat with your grandmother."

"Anything I can help you with?"

"Well, you said you just…And your granny made it clear she wasn't pleased that I…Oh, I'm done here." Mr. Bunsen turned toward his car parked curbside.

"I'll see you tomorrow then," Marty said with a wink. Surely, Mr. Bunsen had encountered the likes of Granny before, or maybe not.

"Yes, tomorrow."

Marty watched Mr. Bunsen hurry to his car. The teacher pushed his remote key, causing it to twitter.

"I've got to get me one of those," Toni murmured under her breath.

"Uh, Toni. We've got a few things to talk about before Mom and Dad get home," Marty said, peering down at his little sister.

* * * * *

Granny entered her bedroom and sat on her bed with a thud.

She worried that Mr. Bunsen's curiosity about Marty could become dangerous. She had known for a while Marty seemed to be developing powers, but she hadn't yet had "the talk" with him. Most members of the Order of Hannibal came into their powers in young adulthood, so she couldn't bring herself to believe that Marty had enough control at this age to tame mosquitoes.

What else can he do? she wondered.

3

GOONS FROM ANOTHER COUNTRY

The silver and black drone, blinking furiously with its green and yellow lights, had returned to its owners soon after Marty harnessed the mosquitoes. The two men huddled over the high-tech wonder. It was small enough not to draw too much attention, with a low hum, and yet it was a powerhouse with its ability to record video and audio. They carefully extracted the recording.

Both men wore ill-fitting clothes, had acne-scarred complexions, and nervous darting eyes.

The taller of the two began to cough, then gingerly handed off the recording to his comrade, who plugged it into an amplified viewing device. The two leaned in, nearly salivating at what they were hearing. Their plan was coming along just fine.

"Following that CRISPR-Cas9 kit delivery to this middle school was genius. Now, we find the right kid for the job," said Tall Cougher.

The shorter man leaned toward him and exhaled heavily, causing Tall Cougher to shield his nose. "You're right, but we're running out of time. We know the data is stored at the International Spy Museum. But, we can't count on it staying there forever."

"The Marty kid looks like our best bet."

"I don't know," said Bad Breath. "What about the big kid, Wade? We can promise him anything he wants. A smart kid like him without any friends should be happy to work with us."

"We need a plan to get the right kid to the museum, and soon. Our comrade needs that CRISPR-Cas9 data."

"I can already see the huge homecoming ceremony and the wads of dough coming our way. All that's standing between us and glory is the security force at that silly spy kid museum."

"Here's what I think we should do…"

4
INTRODUCING THE CLASS HERO OF
WINDSOR MIDDLE SCHOOL

"**D**id Aisha really say that, or is Michael just running his mouth again?" Marty asked between bites of pizza. Michael and Christopher sat among a cafeteria full of their 7th grade classmates, many engrossed in conversation while simultaneously cramming their mouths full of slices of greasy pizza, breadsticks, burgers, chicken fingers, and other kid-friendly food stuffs.

"He swears it's the truth," said Christopher, chewing with his mouth open. The kid from the next table was flexing his hands to imitate a closing door, throwing a hint. "When has Michael ever lied?" he asked.

"Well, there was that time he told Travis he had left the bullfrog outside. It wasn't until the middle of the night that Travis learned he had a roommate. *Ribbit. Ribbit,*" Marty mimicked, laughing.

"Ok, beside that time," Christopher said. "If you don't believe me, ask him yourself."

Michael placed his tray on the table next to Marty's and slid onto the chair. "Man, I'm starving. I hope this pizza isn't greasy."

"No, it's all right."

"It's the bomb," Marty said. "Hey, Christopher was just telling me you had a little chat with Aisha."

"I'll say," Michael said, "About somebody we both know very well."

"Who?" Marty asked.

"You!" yelled Christopher and Michael in unison. High fives all around.

"OK, Michael. Give it up. What exactly did she say about me?" Marty asked, leaning in.

"You're not wearing a wire, are you?"

Marty sheepishly reached under his clothes and yanked off the wire he was wearing. He had pressed "record" when Michael approached the table. He got busy erasing the recording.

"All cleaned up," Marty said. "Let's have it."

"In exchange for this information, you have to let me borrow your door stop alarm."

"Oh, come on," Marty said. "Buy your own."

"Guess you don't need the information," Michael said, pouting and drawing his fingers across his face, sealing his lips.

"Fine. Stop by after school and pick it up. What did Aisha say?"

Michael wiped his chin. "Only that she couldn't believe how heroic you were on the first day of school. To hear her tell it, you saved the whole school from ruin! Geez. The girl acts like you should get a Congressional medal for bravery or something. I told her you already have a medal, a medal for spy kids..."

Marty sprang out of his chair. "You didn't!"

"Man, relax," Michael chuckled. "I'm just playing with you. I just listened to her talk, and then she asked me if I could tell you she likes you. I tell you, the taste of some people..."

"Marty! You're in, man. Michael's given you the hook up!" Christopher yelled, slapping Marty on the back.

Marty broke into a huge grin that quickly turned to a look of fear. He knew he'd have to face Aisha in tomorrow's science class. The beads of sweat on his forehead and nervous laughter matched the tightness in his stomach.

* * * * *

Marty had a sleepless night. He was fascinated by the CRISPR-Cas9 research. He quickly discovered that scientists all over the world were salivating over the kit that gave them the ability to tinker with genomes. Mosquito research meant the possibility of not only sterilizing females, but getting rid of malaria once and for all. Also, the DNA of human cells could be changed. Nevertheless, scientists were working hard to prevent careless tinkering that could lead to super-humans or designer babies.

Marty had fallen asleep imagining all the possibilities. He dreamt about bad guys claiming CRISPR-Cas9 for themselves, shooting anyone who stood in their way with super-powerful machine guns, and selling valuable gene-editing technology secrets to evil countries.

I don't know what Mr. Bunsen has planned, but we sure are lucky to get in on this CRISPR-Cas 9 research, Marty thought as he opened his eyes the next morning. He bounded out of bed without waiting for his alarm clock, and minutes later, met Christopher just outside his front door.

"What do you think Mr. Bunsen has planned for us today?" Christopher asked.

Marty absently scratched a bite on his arm. "As long as it doesn't involve free-flying mosquitoes, I'm in."

Minutes later, they were walking into their science classroom. Mr. Bunsen quickly took attendance, then stood up in front of the entire class, thanking Marty for his heroic actions of the previous day. Marty couldn't believe it.

He snuck a glance at Aisha. Yep, she was eyeing him like he was best friends with Justin Bieber and had backstage passes to the singer's next concert. But, he wasn't and he couldn't. So, she must really be into me. *Me. Marty,* he thought, smiling to himself.

Just as he began to soak in his classmates' applause, the fire alarm sounded.

"Follow me, class," Mr. Bunsen said and herded the class out the door.

"Good old Principal Smiley. It's just my luck that he would spring a fire drill on us when all eyes are on me, and most importantly, Aisha's," Marty mumbled.

Aisha managed to walk out next to him. "That was such a brave thing you did yesterday," she said. "It kind of made for a memorable first day."

"Yeah, I, uh, well..." Marty stammered, as Aisha ran to catch up with a girlfriend.

Christopher moved up next to Marty, poking him in the ribs. "That was smooth."

Marty longingly watched Aisha, who was already several people ahead of him. He kicked himself for missing his big moment. He thought about impressing her with his knowledge about the battle over CRISPR-Cas9. Maybe she hadn't heard that several scientists involved in advancing the new gene-editing technique were now starting companies to make money based on the new technology. And this has global implications! He again wondered what would happen if the technology got into the wrong hands? Or the wrong country.

5
MARTY'S SUPERHERO IDOLS

Marty sighed heavily and looked around his bedroom. His locked spy chest was still intact with his extensive collection of spy gear, minus the door alarm he had loaned Michael. Nearly every inch of wall space was filled with pictures of famous superheroes, ranging from Spiderman, Superman, to Black spy legends Josephine Baker, Odell Bennett Lee, and Harriet Tubman.

Yes, *that* Harriet Tubman, Marty had informed Christopher when he had helped to mount the poster on his wall. In one of Marty's visits to the International Spy Museum website, he had been surprised to find that the woman he learned about in social studies had also been a spy for the U.S. government. How do you lead at least seventy slaves from the South to freedom in the North through the so-called "Underground Railroad" and find time to spy? He had been fascinated with her ever since. His granny, the history buff, was thrilled with his interest.

Marty sat at his desk in front of his bedroom computer scrolling through the web pages of the Spy Museum. He visited the "Shop Gadgets" section, marveling at the selection. A whirlwind of pink entered his room.

"Toni, I'm busy," Marty said.

"You don't look busy to me," Toni said, twirling a pigtail. "What 'cha looking at?"

"Don't worry about it," Marty said, clicking off, but not before she caught a glimpse of a stealth secret sound amplifier.

"Can you buy me a stealthy secret ampi?" Toni said. "Can you please, please?"

"Toni, Mommy just bought you the peanut butter safe. Be happy with that for a while."

"But look at all you have, Marty. The night goggles, the door alarm, the wire, camera tie, fingerprint kit, the thing that makes your voice sound funny…"

"I gave you the camera tie. You used it more than I did. And the what?" Marty asked, getting in Toni's face. "Have you been snooping around my room, again?"

"Not me," she answered quietly. "I think I dreamed it!"

"Yeah, right. How do you know about the voice changer? I'm going to tell Mommy. You can forget your sleepover this weekend," Marty said.

"No, Marty. Don't, don't," she pleaded, grabbing his arm.

Marty looked into her puppy-dog eyes. "Ok, not this time. But, if you do it again, Toni...I'm not kidding..."

"I won't do it again. I promise!" Toni skipped out of his room, hiding her crossed fingers behind her back.

Marty watched her leave, smiled and shook his head. Little sisters. He pulled out his smartphone and spoke into it. The phone started writing a text addressed to Christopher. He pressed Send. In seconds, his smartphone rang.

"Christopher, what good is a text if you pick up the phone and call me every time?"

Christopher defended himself on the other side of the call.

"Listen, buddy. The Museum has the spy video car back in stock. I need you to put up half the money."

"Half? Are you crazy?" Christopher yelled.

"You know you want to use it. Besides, I'm broke after buying the camera tie. I wasn't getting my money's worth out of that one. A 12-year-old looks a little conspicuous in a tie."

"Like you didn't see that one coming. I told you," Christopher said.

"All right, all right. Are you in or not?" Marty asked.

Silence on the other end of the line. Marty could hear Christopher breathing. "What are you going to use it for?"

"Lots of stuff, of course. But initially, we use it for 'Operation Aisha.'"

"What the heck is Operation Aisha?"

"Now you know I have to validate what Michael said. And there's only one way to do that."

"I would have a best friend with a screw loose. Why don't you just ask her like a normal kid?"

"Too easy," Marty said dismissively. "Besides, this will be lots more fun. All we have to do is sneak the video car next to her lunch table. You know how girls talk. If she's thinking about me, she'll say something. And then, I'm in. No more worries. I'll know for sure."

"Just take Michael's word for it and save us the money."

"You know I can't roll like that, Christopher, buddy. Come on, you're my guy. Don't leave me hanging. By myself, it will take me months to get the money."

"How much is it?"

"Marty!" a loud voice called from the other room.

"I gotta go. Mom's looking for me. Thanks, buddy, for having my back!"

"But, I didn't say..." Christopher stopped in mid-sentence as the click of the phone echoed in his ear.

6
GRANNY & THE ORDER
OF HANNIBAL

G ranny looked up at Marty's dad, her son-in-law, as he towered over her. They stood side by side in the family room. She was already dressed in her workout clothes and warmups.

Granny had been going to her aerobics class twice a week since before Marty and Toni were born. The classes kept her limber. She enjoyed getting down on her hands and knees chasing after Toni or Marty and their latest gadget.

Marty's dad kissed her on the forehead. "You be careful with those leg lifts. I don't want you laid up or using a walker the next time I see you."

Granny laughed. "There's nothing our instructor can throw at me that I can't handle. You should come join me some evening, Larry."

"No, thanks. I don't need to embarrass myself trying to keep up with little old ladies in spandex and headbands."

"You're right about that. The ladies could teach you a thing or two. Let me get out of here before they start without me," Granny said, gathering her keys. "The girls will all wonder where I am."

Granny grabbed her bag and was out the door. In no time, she was at the fitness club. She enjoyed the club's location just minutes from the house. It was large enough to provide a variety of choices in group exercises, but small enough to get to know members.

She usually parked as close as possible to the door. On this night, the parking lot was already pretty full, so she pulled into a secluded area far away from the door she usually entered. She was in a hurry, so she didn't notice the young man dressed all in black until he was standing directly behind her.

"Give it up and there won't be any trouble," the husky voice said.

The tiny hairs on Granny's neck stood up. She whirled to face a young man with ashy coloring and a pock-marked complexion. He held one hand in his jacket pocket as if wielding a gun.

"I'm just going to my aerobics class. Now get out of my way and there won't be any trouble," Granny said slowly and evenly.

The young man stared at her in amazement. "I guess you didn't hear me, old lady. Let me spell it out for you. I've got a weapon and I'm not afraid to use it."

Granny looked around. The area was empty. She guessed that all her friends were already inside. She was grateful for that. She touched her hand to her heart, her fingers lightly dancing on the badge pinned to her warmups.

Before the young man knew what was happening, the pavement under his feet seemed to ripple. He lost his balance, and landed heavily on the ground. Granny kicked at his jacket, displaying his "weapon." It was a plastic toy gun. She shook her head slowly, and looked down upon him.

"I have a couple of grandchildren. And, if either one of them ever did what you just tried to do, I would be ashamed. You are disgracing your family. Now, you listen to me. When I walk into that building, get the heck out of here, and don't let me see you around here anymore." Granny turned on her heels and calmly strode toward the building without looking back.

The would-be robber sat on the pavement where he had landed. Dazed. A minute passed. Granny entered the building. The only thing visible was the would-be robber's dark jacket flapping in the wind as he high-tailed it in the opposite direction.

Granny patted her badge. Once again, her Order of Hannibal medal hadn't let her down.

* * * * *

Granny greeted her friends, with no evidence of her encounter with the young thug. She placed her duffle bag in a corner and took her usual spot next to her friend, Janet.

"Good to see you. How's your granddaughter, Aisha?" asked Granny.

"Oh, she's great. She's all excited about 7th grade and her new advanced science class. If there's one thing that keeps that child busy for hours, it's science," said Janet.

There were twenty ladies in all. Each of them sported the same colorful badge Granny wore. The music began and the Order of Hannibal, now transformed into the Senior Ladies Aerobics Club, got underway.

7
MARTY AND THE JET SKI CAPER

Marty sat at the kitchen table piling on the toppings. Cookie-dough ice cream was his favorite. Tonight, Mom had really outdone herself. In addition to the usual hot fudge topping, she had purchased a variety of his favorites for the ice cream sundaes. Colorful sprinkles, marshmallows, pecans, maraschino cherries, and of course, real whipped cream.

The plan was for each family member to choose his or her own, but of course, Marty couldn't help but liberally pile on a mountain of goodies, salivating heavily at the treat inches away from his face.

"Marty's a pig. Leave some for me," Toni wailed.

"Marty!" his mom protested.

Marty's dad walked into the room. He eyed his son's melting masterpiece of ice cream. Toppings began to trickle down.

"Come on now, it's time to start thinking about swim class. You know you've got to get in shape. You're going to be in a whole lot of pain once Coach Jackson gets his hands on you," Marty's dad said.

Marty continued stuffing his mouth, too much in the moment to worry about later consequences.

* * * * *

The next day, Marty sat on the bench poolside, gasping for air along with the rest of Coach Jackson's victims...er...swimmers. He looked around at his classmates. Sammy, a skinny kid, was the only one who didn't seem to be winded at all. *Show-off,* Marty thought.

Marty's interest in swimming had started early. He had begun taking lessons when he was a toddler and Coach Jackson noticed his parents couldn't get him out of the pool following swim class.

"That boy's a natural," Marty's dad had said, patting his son on the head.

So, Marty began swimming on Coach Jackson's club teams until 6th grade, when his time became more and more occupied with his spy gadgets and science experiments. These days, his only swimming came during swim classes and summer break.

"Who didn't get the memo?" Coach Jackson bellowed. "I told you to get into the Bananas program or join up at your local Y. How many of you did that? Not many, from the looks of it."

Marty looked around and saw one kid raise his hand. Yes, it was Sammy. He exchanged glances with Christopher, who was breathing just as hard as he was.

"Two-minute break, then I want you to do six laps," Coach Jackson yelled.

"Six laps?" Marty groaned.

"What's that, Marty?" Coach Jackson asked.

"Nothing, Coach. Happy to do it."

A couple of minutes later, the door to the pool opened and in came three girls, giggling. As they took seats in the bleachers, Marty noticed Aisha was among them. He gave Christopher a long look, and nodded toward the girls. Coach Jackson followed Marty's eyes to the bleachers.

"How about if you lead us off, Marty? Into the pool."

Marty stood up, slowed his breathing, and poked out his chest as he headed for the pool. He was followed by a line of skinny youth with heaving chests.

He glanced again at Aisha. Her eyes followed Marty. *Maybe Michael was telling the truth,* Marty thought, his heart beginning to pump a bit faster. *Why else would she be here?* Or.... his face sank. *Maybe Aisha isn't here to see me after all. Maybe there is another member of the team she has her sights set on.*

"That would be just my luck. Well, I'll show her," Marty mumbled to a puzzled Christopher.

Marty worked on his full-arm extensions and used his over-sized feet to his advantage. He imagined himself in the Olympics and began to swim as if it were the race of his life. He thought back to all that Coach had taught them last year and poured his heart into it.

Marty noticed the kid who had practiced over the summer was smoking most of his classmates. "Smoking Sammy," Marty dubbed him. Leaving everyone else behind. He knew Aisha was watching. Marty began to panic. *That's the kid she came to see! Michael was wrong! She doesn't like me after all.*

"Out of the water!" Coach bellowed. "Two minute break, then eight more laps."

Groans, but shared relief at the short break sounded throughout the room. Aisha was staying put. Marty had an idea. He corralled Christopher in a corner as soon as he came out of the water.

"Meet me in the boys' locker room," said Marty, grabbing his towel from poolside.

"I don't need to go," Christopher protested.

"Look, I don't have time to explain, just meet me," Marty said with urgency.

He saw Christopher's double-take, but he followed his buddy just the same. Marty raced into the boys locker room, grabbed his phone and led a wide-eyed Christopher into an alcove.

"I need you to provide cover for me," Marty said. "We don't have much time. I'll explain later." He located his app on his phone and quickly selected a jet pack.

Christopher looked on. "What are you doing?"

"No time to explain," Marty said, and hurriedly raced back toward the pool. His colorful beach towel shielded the small jet pack. Coach was yelling at them to join the others in the water. Marty and Christopher both jumped in. Marty had pointed his phone at the water and rolled it into the towel before setting it aside.

A low murmur began. Marty grabbed the handle of the jet pack, too small for others to notice, but big enough to give him the extra propulsion he needed. He was zipping past the other swimmers, including "Smoking Sammy." It was all Marty could do to keep from waving and doing tricks. In his mind, he was in the clear blue water of the Caribbean and Aisha was waiting for him ashore, eyes glued on his every move.

Marty didn't see the kid coming. In fact, he did not even know anyone else was around. It wasn't until he had the dazed feeling of falling on his head that he realized he had collided. The jet pack vanished. It took him a minute or two to recover enough to realize he was underwater and needed to resurface.

By that time, Coach had dived into the water, grabbed Marty, and swam to the surface.

"Come on, hurry it up!" Coach yelled. The next thing Marty knew, he was bound tightly with safety straps, and couldn't move his body or head. His swim mates were all standing over him with worried looks on their faces.

"Call 911!" someone shouted.

Marty wondered what Aisha was thinking.

* * * * *

Marty opened his eyes to glaring, bright lights. He squinted and moaned. He figured he had passed out from embarrassment. *Who passes out when his girl is watching? Did I just think of Aisha as my girl?* he asked himself. He closed his eyes, and didn't open them again until he sensed someone hovering over him—Mom and Dad.

"Where am I?" Marty asked, taking in the dour, puke-green-colored walls of the hospital room. He traced the beeping sound to a machine displaying his vitals. It was connected to the IV in his arm.

"Son, son, are you all right?" his dad asked worriedly. "You're at the hospital. You had an accident. Don't you remember?"

"One of the other swimmers ran into you," Marty's mom chimed in. "The doctor made sure you didn't have a concussion. You don't. Still, he advised us to keep you here overnight for observation."

"Oh," Marty groaned.

"Does it hurt?" both parents asked in unison.

"It's not my head I'm concerned about," Marty said.

Marty's parents exchanged glances. Mrs. Hayes, Marty's mom, poked her husband and smiled. "It's Aisha."

"How do you know about that?" Marty asked, rising up. His mom's hands gently pushed him back to the bed.

"Easy. Christopher told us, of course," she said.

Marty frowned.

"Don't go blaming Christopher. He wanted us to know you were a bit distracted and that's why you didn't see your classmate coming."

Marty's dad began to chuckle. "Girl trouble already. And definitely the wrong kind when the girl lands you in the hospital."

Marty's mom began to giggle, then saw her son's look of dismay.

"Sorry, baby. We're just so relieved you're going to be all right," she said.

8

GRANNY DECIDES IT'S TIME FOR "THE TALK"

G ranny looked around her friend Janet's kitchen, took a deep breath and sipped on her coffee. She fingered her medal. It had been handed down to her by her mother. The circle showed the symbol of the Order of Hannibal and the family crest had become a bit banged up over the years. Happily, the medal's effectiveness was as strong as always.

"I wear it every day. I didn't think I'd ever have to use it again," she sighed. "The world has become such a dangerous place. What if that man had attacked somebody else leaving the gym? Somebody not in the Order?"

Janet, who was also the group's aerobics instructor, shook her head. "He didn't, and that's what matters. We've been given a gift and sometimes we have to use it. For good. Nothing wrong with that."

They sat in silence for a moment.

"I'm worried my grandson has them," Granny mumbled.

"The powers?" Janet whispered, touching her Order of Hannibal badge. It was identical to Granny's, except for the addition of her own family crest.

"I've suspected it since he was a baby. The powers turn up differently in everyone. Marty has a fascination with drawing figures and spy equipment. One day, he's likely to put all that to use. I just hope he's ready when the opposition comes," Granny said.

"Marty's a good boy. Are you worried he's going to misuse his gift?"

"I'm concerned he's too young to really know what he's messing with. I'm sure, like me, he's used it in some frivolous ways that no one really knows about. I can remember him experimenting a bit when he was younger. Then he lost interest. Spy gadgets were more interesting."

"So maybe you've got a while, Louise," Janet said.

"I had a recent talk with his science teacher. Marty may be trying out his powers. The more you use them, the more fascinated you become. It's a tempting thing. Most of us find out the hard way," Granny said. She set her cup down. "I always thought it would be my granddaughter. Boys can be so reckless."

"With the mixing of genes, you just never know which grandchild will get it. You know that," Janet said.

"Indeed," Granny said.

"Wait, this isn't just about Marty, is it? You're thinking back on how you got started, aren't you? Don't tell me you have any regrets," Janet said. "Why, Dr. King would not have accomplished all he did without you running interference! And what about that time Ruby Bridges was trying to integrate that school in New Orleans? The little girl was only six years old and there she was at the forefront of the Civil Rights movement!"

"Well, no regrets there," Granny said, leaning back in her chair. "I couldn't just sit by on the sidelines with all that going on. But, I didn't do it all alone. There were members of the Order, black and white, who came into our own during the Civil Rights movement. I just stepped into the void. Right place. Right time."

"It was more than that, I feel," Janet grabbed Granny's hands. "It was destiny. There's some reason for all of this. Marty will find his purpose in time. It will all work out, you'll see."

Granny felt comforted by her friend's words. She let her mind wander over all the times she had used her powers and all the times she had tried to hide her specialness from everyone during her youth.

* * * * *

When Granny arrived home, she said good night to her daughter, the only family member still awake, and went upstairs to her bedroom. She spent a moment gazing at her medal and carefully laid it on her nightstand.

Granny's dreams that night were filled with actions she took during the Civil Rights movement. With her ability to move pavement, she had kept several people out of harm's way as angry bullets flew in their direction, dogs nipped at their heels, and jail doors closed on them, unjustly.

She had comforted Dr. Martin Luther King, Jr. the night he wrote his famous *Letter from the Birmingham Jail.* Dr. King led many protests in the South during the 1960s, and would sometimes get jailed for acting on his beliefs. Granny was one who had joined him in the fight for equality for all, using her special powers.

She fell asleep with a smile on her lips. She thought of what her grandson, named after one of the most influential Americans of all time and his own grandad, one of the famous Tuskegee airmen of World War II, could accomplish with the right focus.

9
MARTY AND CHRISTOPHER PLAN A POWER TEST

M r. Bunsen was giving final instructions for the night's homework. The class was instructed to view a CRISPR-Cas9 YouTube video by Dr. Jennifer Doudna and come prepared to summarize how the gene editing technology could potentially provide a cure for genetic disorders.

When Mr. Bunsen finished describing the assignment, along with the rest of the class, Marty and Christopher headed for the door. Christopher began to walk ahead.

"Wait up!" Marty called.

But, he kept walking and didn't slow his steps. Marty ran after Christopher and grabbed his arm, confronting him. "What's up with you?" he asked.

"Man, I'm glad you're all right and all. I thought we were best friends. But, you've been holding out. I don't even know who you are anymore."

"What are you talking about?"

"You know what I'm talking about. The jet pack. How the heck did you conjure that up? Do you want me to announce it to the whole school?"

Quickly, Marty pulled Christopher into a janitor's closet.

"Listen, I don't how to explain this," Marty told his friend. "The truth is I'm trying to figure it all out myself. I'm lucky I only gave myself one day in the hospital. All I know is I have this...ability."

Christopher shifted his backpack. "How the heck did you do that? And what else can you do? My best friend is freaking Spiderman and he doesn't even tell me!"

"Whoa. Spiderman I am not. Something special perhaps, but Spiderman, no," Marty said with a grin. Suddenly turning serious, he leaned in to his friend. "This is wild, incredible, but pretty scary, man. I haven't really figured it out."

"I know!" Christopher yelled. "We need an Olympics. A Marty Olympics!"

Marty screwed up his face. "Now you've really lost it. What the heck are you talking about?"

"Let's figure out what you can do, what your powers are, what your limits are. You never know when you may need to use them. For legal stuff, of course," Christopher quickly added.

"Of course," Marty agreed. "I learned my lesson. No more spur-of-the-moment inventions to impress a girl. Even if it is Aisha…"

Suddenly the door swung open. It was a school janitor. Upon seeing the flushed faces of two teen boys, his eyes locked on theirs and he slowly shook his head.

"It's not what you think!" Christopher protested.

He and Marty took off at a fast walk as the janitor stared after them. "Don't let me catch you in here again!" he yelled.

10
TONI DIPS INTO MARTY'S SPY BOX

Toni gleefully laughed as she played outside her home with Chez Vous. Despite his small size, the family's fluffy Bichon had a deathly grip on the red rubber pull toy. She detected a low hum and turned her head toward the sky. She squinted at the sun.

At first, Toni couldn't make it out, then noticed a silver and black drone with flashing green and yellow lights hovering just above the trees. Chez Vous growled with the pull toy spilling out of his mouth. As she looked away, the drone took off at high speed.

"That's enough, Chez Vous. We need a snack," Toni announced. She grabbed the toy one last time and they headed inside. Once she had gotten an apple for herself, and a Milkbone for the dog, Toni bounded upstairs. She walked past Marty's room, then slowed her steps. After a moment, she hurriedly kept walking, only to turn back around seconds later.

"I promised not to take Marty's things," she murmured. "I promised not to take anything. I promised not to keep it. I can't get in trouble for borrowing."

Toni tiptoed over to a large box filled with Marty's spy treasures. To her dismay, she found it securely locked. She pouted. As she abruptly turned to leave, she tripped and fell onto the box, causing a trick lid to flip open. Inside was a small cavity containing a credit card lock picking kit. Toni set to work.

"I've seen this on the spy cartoons," she said, surprised that after just a few tries, she was able to open the box.

Her eyes widened. She had stumbled upon the mother lode. Toni couldn't have been happier if she had found a truckload of chocolate cupcakes. And like most kids, she loved her chocolate.

Toni lost track of time. She had sent the video camera car for a run down the long hallway separating her room from Marty's. She heard voices downstairs.

"What's wrong, Chez Vous?" Marty asked.

Chez Vous barked enthusiastically.

"That's one crazy dog," Christopher said.

Toni frantically threw all the items strewn about on the floor into the box and pointed the remote toward the car to bring it back.

Just as footsteps sounded on the stairs, the car zipped into Marty's room. Toni sent it under the bed, and accidentally pushed the record button. She quickly locked up and ran into the hallway. With her heart beating, she met the boys, hiding the remote behind her back.

"Hi, Christopher. Hi, Marty. What are you doing?" she asked innocently.

The boys peered at her. "What are you up to?" Marty asked, leaning down so they were now nose to nose. "You haven't been taking my stuff, have you? You know what will happen if you do."

"I haven't been keeping your stuff," Toni said. She turned on her heels and headed to her room, still shielding the remote.

"I haven't been keeping your stuff," Christopher mimicked.

Marty shook his head. He and Christopher fell on his bed, laughing.

"I just need to get my phone, then we'll go test it out," Marty said.

The light on the camera car blinked silently, recording every word.

"Man, this could be awesome. Maybe you're the next Iron Man, Superman, Green Lantern, Black Lightning...Who knows, your powers could be more awesome than any of them!"

"Slow your roll, Christopher. Let's just take this one step at a time....Hold on a minute."

Marty walked into the hallway and peered around, making sure Toni was nowhere in sight. Satisfied, he walked back to his room, and flopped back on the bed. Just a few feet away lay the unlocked spy box.

"Let's think about what we need to test," Marty said. "Let's focus on stuff to show how strong my powers may be."

Christopher's eyes grew round. "Let's have you draw a ball of fire and see if that comes to life. Next, a Ferrari, a real Lamborghini..."

"Wait, this isn't like rubbing a genie lamp and getting everything you wish for. This is about seeing what I can do, remember?" Marty said.

"Ok, think back. What have you done so far? And how long did the creation last?" Christopher asked.

Marty thought for a second, then jumped up. "Let's go."

* * * * *

Toni heard the boys run downstairs and leave out the front door. It was her big chance. She ran upstairs with Chez Vous at her heels. She raced back to the video camera car and played back the audio. Toni couldn't believe what she heard. Her brother, Marty, with some sort of powers? How was that even possible?

She played the recording again and again. Her eyes widened and she immediately thought of telling Granny or her parents. Then she remembered she would get into trouble for prying. And worse, Marty would never trust her again. Maybe her brother was onto her and thought this was a good way to get back at her. It would be just like him to pretend he had some earth shattering news to get her all excited.

Toni lay on Marty's bed for a long while, staring at the ceiling. She gave a big sigh, stood up, and gave the sign for sealing her lips, quietly replaced the car in the spy box, locked it, and went downstairs.

11
SUPERPOWER TEST DAY

Marty and Christopher walked the few blocks to the school playground armed with a few tricks. Marty clutched his smartphone with its drawing apps, and a few spy gadgets.

Christopher jumped up and down with excitement.

"OK, I've created dogs, little dogs, various domestic animals, bicycles, model cars. But I've haven't gone large...." Marty said.

"What about a lion or tiger?" Christopher asked, practically drooling.

"There's only one problem with that, buddy."

"What's that?"

"What if I can't get the lion back in the cage?"

"Only one way to find out," Christopher said.

Marty took a good look around and decided the area was vacant. He slowly pulled his phone out of his pocket and opened a drawing app. He pointed to a lion and began to imagine it. After a minute, he turned to Christopher.

"OK, so I'll imagine it a bit small," he said. "Not that that is going to do us any good if this gets out of control. Just stand back a bit. I'll focus on where I want it to materialize and I'll contain it, if we're lucky." Marty said the last bit under his breath, along with a quick prayer.

He had spent a lot of time at the zoo and figured if a lion could tear up a piece of meat in seconds, how long would it take to devour two skinny 7th graders?

He closed his eyes and pointed the phone in front of him.

A soft roar went up. Marty and Christopher in-stinctively jumped. The lion wasn't much of a lion at all. In fact, it was a cub. The wobbly cub took a step or two, and then seemed to slow down and stretch.

The boys were speechless and too rooted in amazement to move. After a leisurely stretch, the li-on turned its head in their direction. Then rolled on the ground as if to scratch its back.

"Some ferocious lion!" Christopher howled.

Marty was frozen in time. He stared at his creation. Sure, it was a cub, and it was kind of cute. *Still*, he thought the cub had teeth. *What if?*

"Make a bigger one!" Christopher called. "This one isn't cooked yet."

Marty went back to work with his phone. Miraculously, the cub disappeared. In its place popped the largest lion the boys had ever seen. They looked at each other in terror. Marty was sure the lion's teeth now on full display as it licked its chops were enormous. He pondered the damage this lion could do, as it began to steadily walk toward them.

"Do something!" Christopher shouted.

"What do you think I'm doing? You're the one who wasn't satisfied with the first one!"

"I said go bigger. I didn't say to create a monster!"

The lion continued to advance. Marty gasped. Only a few feet separated the wild animal from the boys. He frantically imagined the lion's disappearance. Just as it was about to pounce, the lion vanished.

The boys fell against each other in relief. Then Christopher punched Marty on the shoulder.

"That was awesome!" he yelled.

"That was ridiculous. I almost pissed my pants," Marty admitted.

"I thought you said you'd done this before?" Christopher said.

"Yeah, with domestic animals. The game changes when you're talking about something that can eat you for breakfast."

"I'll say," Christopher agreed. "Man, just think what you can do with this!"

Marty shrugged his shoulders. He was just beginning to fully imagine the possibilities. Truth was, he had been spooked by the lion, and it wasn't until he had reined it back in that he knew for sure he could. He shuddered to think what their fate could have been. Worse, he couldn't imagine living with the guilt of losing his best friend since kindergarten.

"I think that's enough for one day. Let's head home," Marty said.

Despite Christopher's protests, they packed up and headed for home. First, Marty had Christopher promise not to tell a soul.

12
MARTY'S CREATIONS
ATTACK BULLY WADE

The next day, when the bell rang, the students of Windsor Middle School poured out of the school doors, happy to reclaim their freedom for a few hours before they had to start all over again. "School is jail," one of Marty's classmates had once said. He never forgot the saying. Each time he thought of it, it made him smile.

Marty couldn't wait to get to school each morning. His love of science kept him interested. *This new mosquito research sounded promising*, he thought. He was so curious about what experiments they would do using the new CRISPR-Cas9 technique. He was thrilled his new science teacher wanted to explore the impact of altering DNA and was willing to work with his 7th grade classroom to do it.

Marty shifted his backpack load, and noticed Aisha. He peered closely. On her heels was, no! It couldn't be. Yes, it was Wade, the bully. And he was taunting Aisha. She was walking quickly, trying to get away. He was relentless, nearly bumped into her, and taunted her.

As they neared, Marty could make out what Wade was saying.

"Aisha and Marty, what a lovely couple. Who knew a guy would knock himself out for you? Wow, you must really be something special. Aisha and Marty. Only you can't have a boyfriend if he drowns himself!" Wade cackled and threw his arms in the air. Aisha darted this way and that, trying to throw him off, without any luck.

Marty stepped in their path. "I think your mom is calling you. Leave her alone, Wade."

Wade stopped and drew up to his full height, towering over Marty. "Oh, look, your boyfriend has come to your rescue, just like in the fairy tale Taylor Swift sings about. I'm going to puke."

"I don't want to have to tell you again Wade, or..."

"Or what?" Wade yelled, getting in Marty's face.

"Or else. You don't want to know."

"Marty, it's OK. Don't fight him," Aisha said in a low voice.

"I've known this bully for a long time. He's all talk, no action. He's…"

Wade took a swing. Marty swung back. Wade lost his balance and fell to the ground. He was getting up to swing at Marty again when the smartphone fell out of Marty's pocket. Marty closed his eyes. When he opened them, a flock of crows came out of nowhere and began nipping at Wade's hair. The other boy frantically waved his arms and his jacket to get the birds off.

"Get off. Get off me!" Wade yelled.

Aisha looked on, astonished. Marty frantically tried to rein the crows back in. It wasn't until they had pecked at Wade, slashing at his hair and skin, drawing blood, that Marty was finally able to get them back.

Wade got up and ran off screaming.

Aisha looked at him and then turned to Marty. "What just happened?"

Marty looked down at his feet. "I, I don't know."

A bunch of kids ran up to them. "Wow! That was awesome!" a small blond boy yelled.

"Yeah, who knew the big, bad bully would be afraid of a few birds?" a kid with black braids and blond tips asked.

Laughter all around. "Yeah, birds that bite."

"Must be that cheap deodorant he wears," the blond boy said. He paused for a moment, and scratched his head. "Funny how the crows only went after Wade."

The kids laughed and walked off, shaking their heads at what they had just witnessed. Aisha looked at Marty. He looked down, and stuffed his phone into his pocket.

"If you like, I can walk you home," Marty said.

Aisha nodded. Marty had to pinch himself to be sure he wasn't dreaming. At that moment, Christopher caught up with them.

"Oh, there you are. I've been looking for you," he said.

Marty tried to subtly give him the nod.

Christopher glanced at Aisha next to Marty. "Oh, hi, Aisha...Say, are we still going to do that thing?" he asked turning toward Marty.

"I'm going to walk Aisha home," Marty said.

Christopher looked back and forth at the two of them. "Oh, sure. I get it. No problem. We'll connect later. Text me. I mean, about the thing, not the walk. I mean..."

"I got it," Marty said, cutting him off. Christopher was going to spoil everything.

Aisha smiled. "Let's go."

Marty was frantically thinking of something to say. He noticed Aisha's fashionable outfit. She always seemed to be dressed so nicely. He couldn't help but notice she was usually dressed in bright purple from head to toe. But, it wasn't in a little girl outfit.

Her knit top came down just to the line of her hip jeans, showing just a bit of skin. Her backpack was a kind of snakeskin purple and decorated with a couple of *Hello Kitty* pins. She was slim, but shapely, and wore boots with a bit of a heel. Still, she was a head shorter than Marty. *Perfect,* he thought.

They walked for blocks without speaking a word. Then suddenly, Aisha turned to Marty. "Why did you come over when you saw Wade bothering me?"

"Because bullies don't have any right to take things out on others to make themselves feel better," Marty promptly replied. Aisha smiled. Marty felt himself blushing and thought this would be a good time to change the subject.

"How do you like our science class?" Marty asked.

"I love it!" Aisha said.

"Did you know CRISPR-Cas9 has also allowed scientists to correct a genetic defect in a type of muscular dystrophy so organs grown in animals won't get rejected when they're ready to transplant them?"

"How do you know all this?"

"I read. My mom's a travel writer, and sometimes, she does some science writing. She's always willing to pass along journals when she's finished."

"Bring it on!" Aisha laughed. "I've loved science since I was a little girl, you know?"

"Yeah, I can say the same. Science rules everything. I love Neil deGrasse Tyson and…"

"And you can save a classroom of students from their teacher, the mad scientist?" Aisha asked. Marty joined the laughter at the expense of Mr. Bunsen. *He deserves it,* Marty thought.

Aisha stopped in front of an attractive ranch-style home with field stones. "This is my stop."

"So soon?" Marty asked. "Is it just you and your parents?"

"And my grandma. Watch out for her now. She can keep up with anybody. We think it's her weekly aerobics class."

"That must be the magic formula. Same with my granny. It takes a lot for her to miss out on her aerobics class. Hey…I wonder if they know each other," said Marty.

"I wonder. Where do you live?"

"Oh, just… totally in the opposite direction," Marty laughed.

"Well, thanks for going out of your way…to walk me home, I mean. And to take on Wade, that was so brave."

"Aw, I've known him since elementary school. You'd think he would have learned his lesson by now."

"I think that's called dense," Aisha said. She tugged at Marty's sleeve. "Thanks again. But don't worry, you don't have to walk me every day."

"Oh, I won't. I mean…unless you want me to…" Marty trailed off.

"Let's play it by ear," Aisha said.

Marty nodded and walked off. After a few steps, he turned to watch Aisha walking up her front stairs. He hoped she would look back. For just a moment, he considered pulling out his phone program and producing something she may like…flowers, a sleek new bike, a jet ski…then he thought better of it. If this was going to happen, it would have to happen naturally.

Still, he spent a restless night wondering just what Aisha meant when she said "Let's play it by ear."

13
MARTY: SOLDIER COMMANDER

Marty and Christopher easily performed laps in the pool. Under the watchful eye of Coach Jackson, Marty had once again become one of the top swimmers. He had gotten into pretty good shape, finding he could manage the laps Coach prescribed without too much effort. He had certainly learned his lesson after the collision at the beginning of the season. No more jet pack hijinks for him.

Besides, now that he and Aisha were getting to know each other, he no longer felt the need to show off. The best thing about their friendship was that it was built on common interests: their love of science and all things spy-related. Marty no longer felt compelled to be someone he wasn't.

Marty felt as comfortable in the water as he did on land. He had first joined a swim team at the local YMCA when he was just six years old. A swim instructor had noticed he didn't want to get out of the water after swim lessons and recommended he join the swim team for his age group. At that age, it was just as much fun for Marty to hang out with his friends on the benches and munch on healthy snacks between heats as it was to swim.

Coach Jackson called for a break, giving Marty and Christopher an opportunity to race each other the length of the pool. Coach Jackson smiled and shook his head, noting on his clipboard how the two had become among the fastest swimmers in the class. He wished Marty was willing to dedicate his time again to join the school's swim team.

* * * * *

Christopher and Marty stood inside the local Best Buy store playing games. Marty's dad had picked them up after school and then decided to make a stop to get a case for his smartphone.

Marty longed for an Xbox One X. He figured he may as well get acquainted with the games so he could make an informed decision when it was time to shop, though that wasn't likely to happen anytime soon. He had been spending every dollar he got on spy equipment for the last several years. His parents refused to allow him to get a job after school, saying it would interfere with his study time.

Marty was thinking about how he'd have to run more errands for his granny if he was going to take Aisha out to the movies when Christopher playfully punched him in the arm. "So did you kiss her?"

"Did I kiss her? Have you been listening to me? She said 'let's play it by ear.' How the heck do you follow that up with a kiss?"

Christopher peered at Marty who was now looking very uncomfortable. He had found a speck of lint on his shirt and was staring intently at it.

"You act like you're scared of girls."

Marty shot Christopher an angry look. "And you're not?"

"Aw, Marty. You came to her rescue. Saved her from big, bad Wade. Why couldn't you seize the moment and lean in for the kiss?" Christopher asked.

"Yeah, right. Enough about that," Marty said. "We need to continue with our testing. But enough with the wild animals," Marty said.

"Aw, man, that was awesome. Ok, I'm with you on that one. You're my buddy, but you're stretching it if you think I'm risking my life for you," Christopher said.

"Tomorrow after school, meet me at the back entrance and let's put it to the test," Marty said.

"Deal."

* * * * *

Christopher joined Marty in lock step right after he exited the school doors.

"I've come up with a short list for us to work through," Marty said. "We need to approach this in a much more scientific manner. Hypothesis, test, record results."

"Sounds good to me," Christopher agreed. "What's first?"

Marty put his arm around his friend's shoulder. "Follow my lead." He took off running at breakneck speed with Christopher laboring to keep up. They tore past several of their classmates, including Wade, who glowered at them as they nearly ran into him.

Marty and Christopher kept running until finally they arrived in a commercial district with huge, ominous-looking buildings all around.

"Where are we?" Christopher asked between gasps.

"Our laboratory," Marty answered, pronouncing the word in syllables, *la-bor-a-to-ry*. "We're going to test inside, under controlled conditions."

Too winded to protest, Christopher meekly followed Marty inside a massive stone building that looked like it had been a manufacturing site long ago. Now, the building sat vacant, looking forlorn in its abandonment.

Marty looked left, then right, and marched up to the huge double doors. Padlocked. Christopher started to ask what's next when Marty produced his lock-picking kit and went to work. Little did he know the kit had been in the hands of his little sister a short while ago.

A minute or two passed, then success! The lock groaned, then popped open reluctantly. Marty whipped out some work gloves, grabbed the rusted lock and slung it aside.

He then reached for the door and opened it enough for the two of them to enter. It was still afternoon so there was enough light for them to make out a vacant space, filled with huge cobwebs and dank smells.

"It stinks in here!" Christopher yelled.

"Do you want to do this?" Marty asked. "We can't test in the comfort of our bedrooms. And you saw what happened in the park. Are you in or not?"

"I'm in," Christopher mumbled.

Marty reached into his backpack and pulled out his phone, his video car, and a tool Christopher hadn't seen before.

"And, what's that?" Christopher asked.

"You'll find out soon enough. Hey, why don't you take a look in the next room and see if there are any electrical outlets while I set everything up?" Marty asked.

Christopher hesitated for a moment, but then decided he'd rather risk whatever ghouls might be hiding around the corner than let on how uncomfortable he felt in the gloomy warehouse.

He wandered off. Marty got to work.

* * * * *

A minute later, Christopher rounded the corner, returning to Marty, at a fast clip.

"Hey, what's wrong with you? There isn't going to be any electricity in this abandoned warehouse. What the … ?"

Christopher stopped in his tracks. There, in front of him, was a soldier. Clad in camouflage with some sort of metallic padding on its shoulders, the soldier stood tall, all four feet of him. Christopher was awestruck. This soldier appeared to be a human-like R2D2. He glanced at Marty, who proudly stood eyeing his creation.

The soldier appeared to be … breathing … and awaiting the next command. And her commander was Marty. Marty's eyes were aglow, relishing the power at his fingertips. His mind raced as he thought of what paces he could put the soldier through. And he also considered what his soldier could do to someone like Wade. If Wade thought the crows were something, wait until he saw what Marty was really capable of.

Marty waved his hands and slowly raised them. Before their eyes, the lone soldier multiplied until the one became many.

Christopher began to count aloud. "One, two, three, four, five, six… There must be a dozen here!"

Marty quickly equipped each soldier with ear-listening devices, goggles, and motion sensors.

Christopher watched as each piece materialized before them.

Marty closed his eyes, then opened them and shouted, "Now go!"

The soldiers formed pairs, setting off on a mission. As they fanned out, Marty set his smartphone stop watch. Then he reached into his backpack and pulled out a small crate filled with white mice.

"Where did you get that?" Christopher asked.

"I could tell you. But, I'd have to kill you. Trust me. It's all in the name of science."

Marty gingerly set the crate down and slid open the latch. Scampering out were the white mice, running this way and that, in every direction. As one left the room they were in, and turned the corner, a soldier darted after. The other soldiers followed suit, marching methodically.

"Let the games begin!" Marty yelled.

Marty and Christopher ran from room to room in the cavernous building, watching from a distance as the soldiers used their equipment to slowly capture the mice.

Marty couldn't believe how the soldiers he had just created, were carefully making their way around the dusty room, focusing in on darting mice, and dashing out to capture them with laser-like precision.

As a mouse tried to make its escape up the wall toward the window, a soldier arched its body and trudged up the wall horizontally to reach the rodent. Frantic squeals revealed the soldier had found its target.

A mouse darted into a hole in a wall, chased by a soldier who simply smashed through and grabbed its target by the tail, bringing down the entire wall. The soldier jumped up victorious, covered in dust and wooden shards.

Minutes passed. The soldiers fell into lock step and returned to the room where they started. Marty gathered the frightened mice one by one and dropped them into the crate, counting them as he did.

"And that one makes twelve. They're all here. How about that, Christopher? What do you say..." Marty asked, stopping as Christopher screamed. A soldier had grabbed his shirt, and was peering at him.

"Hey! Let me go!" Christopher yelled.

Marty screamed. The soldier released him.

"So, there's a defect," Marty said, shrugging his shoulders. "We'll fix it and tomorrow, we'll send them up the Sears Tower!"

14
AISHA AND HER NEWFOUND POWERS

Aisha quietly raised her bedroom window and climbed through, lowering herself onto the grass of her backyard. She looked up, noticing the moon was just a sliver of light. Just what she was hoping for. She had pored through her science books, but hadn't yet come across anything to explain why her eyesight seemed to be getting so...strong.

Aisha was usually afraid of the dark, but was losing her fear and noticing things in the dark no one else did. The possums that scampered about playing tag. The owl that swooped here and there, either looking for food or testing its wings. The couple who left home clad all in black, apparently looking to blend in rather than stand out in the reflective jackets most neighborhood night-walkers wore.

She pulled her jacket tighter around her and looked across the yard. A toad caught her attention. She easily followed its path in the near-pitch-black darkness. She smiled when the toad crossed the path of a rabbit, which hesitated only a few moments before resuming its trek through the wooded area behind her home.

Suddenly, she saw movement and quickly made out the contrasting black and white colors of a skunk. She halted and held her breath.

"I'm not a threat," Aisha said aloud.

To her relief, the skunk continued on its way. After a few moments more, Aisha noticed a flock of bats swooping down near the ground, aiming for something. And though they should have been quite invisible in the darkness, she could make out a sheen to their bodies. *Mosquitoes,* she marveled.

Aisha spent the next hour walking through her neighborhood and adjacent neighborhoods, criss-crossing back and forth through the suburb's wooded areas. Outside of night creatures, she hadn't encountered anyone who could possibly give her secret away.

Aisha glanced at her watch as she started her climb back through the window. With her heart pounding, she had ventured into neighborhoods that would have normally been off-limits to her without an adult present. Her night vision made her feel prepared to handle anything.

If anyone with bad intentions headed toward her, she figured she could run away before he got too close or zig-zag away until he lost sight of her. *It's undeniable*, Aisha thought. *I've developed night vision without the aid of anything artificial. I can see in the dark.*

15
TONI NABS MARTY'S SPY MANUAL

Toni pedaled her flaming pink bicycle with its flowing streamers through her neighborhood. Her matching helmet and outfit brought smiles to the faces of passing drivers. She stopped at a friend's house, discovered her friend wasn't home, and took off for the park alone. As she parked her bike and jumped onto a swing, a burly, mousy-haired boy headed her way. To her surprise, he got into the swing next to her.

"Hey, you're Marty's sister, aren't you?" he asked.

"Yeah. Do you know Marty?" Toni asked.

"You might say that. We're kind of like the best of friends."

"Then why haven't I seen you before at our house? Christopher is like his best-est friend and he's there all the time," Toni said.

"Aw, Chris. I know him, too. The three of us have classes together."

"What's your name? I'm Toni."

"Wade. Nice to meet you."

"Nice to meet you, too."

"You know, Toni. It's a good thing you're seeing me this week," Wade said.

"Why?"

"Because I'm working with some guys and for a little bit of work, they're giving me smartphones to give out to my friends."

"Smartphones!" Toni yelled. "I love smartphones! Only I can't get one. Daddy says it's too expensive. It's not fair because Marty has one."

"How would you like your own, Toni?" Wade smiled his Cheshire cat smile. "It's simple. Here's what I need you to do."

* * * * *

Toni crept up the stairs without anyone in the house noticing her. Chez Vous startled her, so she figured someone else in the house had let him out. She had to hurry. Marty adored his spy manual. He had used it for years, and never seemed to tire of it. Toni knew it contained information Marty would use to concoct his spy escapades, and to daydream of having a career as a secret service agent, or whatever it was he wanted to be when he grew up.

Focus. Focus, she told herself. *I'm on a spy mission. My mission is to get the spy manual and deliver it to Wade in the park before anyone catches on.* And just beyond her reach was her very own smartphone. That's if she could pull off this mission properly.

Quick. I've got to be quick. Toni fumbled with the lock pick kit until she again found a tool that would work. When the lock sprang open, she breathed a deep sigh of relief, grabbed the spy manual and stuffed it in the backpack she had grabbed when she entered the house. Just as her mom turned the corner, Toni dashed out the door. Her short legs pumped as fast she could go, carrying her back to the park where a shiny new phone awaited her.

When she came into sight, Wade stood up from the sandbox where he had been chuckling and running sand through his fingers.

"What a pushover," he said softly. "Clueless little girls will do anything for a smartphone. This is too easy." He wiped the smirk off his face as Toni pedaled up.

"Did you get it?" he asked.

"Oh, yeah. I almost got caught by my mom, but I made it out OK," Toni said, almost out of breath. She yanked off her backpack and pulled out the coveted spy manual.

"Let me see that." Wade grabbed the manual, and began paging through it with glee. "Yep, looks like it's all here. Thanks."

As he headed to his bike, Toni yelled. "Hey! What about my phone?"

"I'm going to get it now," Wade said, pedaling away. "Just give me a few minutes. I couldn't go running around with a smartphone. I didn't know I was going to run into anyone to give it to. And don't worry, I'll return the spy manual when I'm done."

Toni sighed and sat down on a swing. The phone would be hers. It seemed she sat in the swing for a long time.

"No Wade." She wasn't sure, but the knot in her stomach told her something wasn't right. "I don't really know that boy. What if he tricked me?" she asked herself.

When Toni finally got back on her bike and headed for home, she pedaled much slowly than she had delivering the spy manual to Wade. She thought of how she didn't have either a smartphone or a spy manual to bring home. When Marty found out about his book, he would be furious.

16

THE ORDER OF
HANNIBAL MEDAL

Just minutes after his new duties as commander-in-chief, Marty was back at home in the kitchen with his mom, munching on banana bread.

"Mom, your banana bread is the best."

"You said that already. Now tell me why you're late getting home from school," she said. She glanced at the kitchen clock. "I don't know what's gotten into you guys. Toni isn't home yet, either. I guess I'm going to have to call her home from the Johnsons."

"Well...I...See, Mom, I..." Marty began, avoiding her gaze. He stalled for time as he weighed his options. One, he could tell her the truth. *I was in an old, abandoned warehouse testing my superpowers.* No good. *I was hanging out at school to see if Aisha was looking for me to walk her home again.* Naw. *I was playing with Christopher and lost track of time.* Not a good idea. He had been warned about that one.

"Mom, I stayed after to get extra help. I want to do well on my science test. We're having it in a few days." *At least it's a half truth,* Marty thought, crossing his fingers behind his back.

"Oh, that's a good idea, Marty," his mom smiled. "Granny said it's a good sign that Mr. Bunsen stopped in to ask how you were doing right after school started. It's good when your teachers take an interest in you. Keep the lines of communication open, and you'll do well in class."

"Yes, ma'am," Marty agreed, stuffing his face, hoping that would put an end to the conversation.

Granny entered the room with a photo album in hand.

"Mom, what are you doing looking at all those old albums?" Mrs. Hayes asked Granny.

"Oh, I started thinking about how Haward loved playing with you kids. With Marty and Toni getting older, I can't help but think about how proud he would have been of his grandchildren, watching them grow up."

Mrs. Hayes smiled and hugged her mom. Marty thought he saw tears in his mom's eyes. His grand-dad had died before he was born. But he often thought of him and wondered what kind of man he had been.

"He was a fine man, indeed," Granny was saying. "Come here, Marty, let me share some of these photos with you."

Marty sighed and stuffed his mouth with his remaining chunk of banana bread. He knew this could take a while. Granny led him to the sofa, where she turned the photo album back to the first page and began describing Marty's granddad to him. She slowly showed him the pages of the album. Marty knew many of these stories by heart. His grandad had been a military brat and his grandad's father was of special pride to the family, as he had been a Tuskegee Airman.

"The Tuskegee Airmen were an elite unit of the Air Force during World War II and are heralded for their service. They were the first African-American aviators in the armed forces," Granny said.

She flipped the page. Marty's eye was drawn to a medal like the one Granny occasionally wore.

"Granny, Granddad had a medal just like yours!" Marty exclaimed. "I thought that was just for the old ladies' aerobics club."

"Senior ladies," Granny corrected him. He thought she looked surprised that Marty had picked the badge out of the photo. It had been a year since he had seen her photo album. He found himself growing more curious about things he hadn't really questioned before.

Marty's granddad stood among several of his dad's former Tuskegee Airman comrades at a reunion party held in public. The medal was clearly visible on the sweater he wore.

"We sometimes dressed alike ... our friends would tease us about it." Marty heard the hesitation in her voice, and noticed his mom giving her a look.

Strange, Marty thought. Granny had a lot of quirks, but running out of things to talk about was not one of them.

17
MOSQUITO HUNTING FIELD TRIP

The Advanced Science 303 classroom was excited Mr. Bunsen had scheduled a field trip. They had learned mosquito research had begun long before CRISPR-Cas9 became well known. Marty was surprised to find out about a Midwestern researcher at a local university, who studied the mating habits of mosquitoes and was using that research to help eradicate the pesky beings from the earth.

Still, CRISPR-Cas9 was a game-changer. Research that normally took decades to make an impact could expect a sped up timetable due to CRISPR's ability to splice out genomes and replace them. Marty knew Aisha was as excited about this as he was.

He also knew Christopher would join them during lunch, but was starting to notice his buddy was a bit quiet when Aisha was around. Marty hoped Christopher would find someone, a special girl like he had. So far, that hadn't happened. Marty made sure to always include Christopher in his lunchtime conversations with Aisha, while sometimes privately wishing they could have time alone.

He acknowledged walking on eggshells around Aisha. As much as he wanted to, he hadn't dared kiss her yet. He told himself the right time would come. Until then, he was having fun spending time with someone who loved science as much as he and Christopher did. And of course, she smelled much better than Christopher. Sorry, the truth is the truth.

"Tell me again why we've got to become human guinea pigs for this science unit," Christopher moaned.

"If you had worn the long sleeves and pants like Mr. Bunsen said rather than a T-shirt and shorts, maybe you wouldn't be roadkill at a mosquito feast right now," Marty reminded him. "We need these mosquitoes."

"I guess I wasn't the only one who didn't get the memo," Christopher said, motioning to several classmates who were also scratching and moaning about their discomfort.

As mosquitoes swarmed overhead, Wade hogged the anti-itch cream. Mr. Bunsen had relented and passed it around, chiding his students who didn't follow instructions for proper attire for the field trip.

"Are there any questions?" Mr. Bunsen asked as the students captured mosquitoes in netting and transferred them to the small jars they had brought along.

"I have one," a small voice said.

Wade giggled and poked a finger in Marty's ribs. "Of course, your smart girlfriend has something to say."

"Cut it out, Wade. It's bad enough you forget to share the anti-itch cream, do we have to listen to your mouth today, too?" Marty asked.

Wade frowned and leaped as if to unleash a punch. Marty didn't flinch.

"Yes, Aisha, what is it?" asked Mr. Bunsen.

"I know the researchers are trying to sterilize eggs by changing their DNA, so even if they mate, it will interfere with the female's ability to lay eggs, but wouldn't they have to go all over the world to sterilize the eggs? That's not very practical, is it?" asked Aisha.

"Great question. Their hypothesis of changing the ability of female mosquitoes to have viable eggs, and instead produce infertile eggs, would cut down on the population. Also, companies could develop a product to affect the DNA of developing eggs in such a way that we can greatly reduce diseases," said Mr. Bunsen.

"You mean like stemming malaria in developing countries," said Marty.

"And other insect-borne diseases, like the Zika virus," added Christopher.

"You're all correct. It's good to see your imaginations firing. There's nothing like a good, old-fashioned field trip into the wild to get the brain working," said Mr. Bunsen smugly. "Let's move on to another area near the river. We can then discuss how these latest advancements will reduce that timetable considerably."

"Oh, great," Wade whined, scratching at the red marks on his arms and legs.

Marty noticed, and he grinned as he walked along with his classmates.

After another hour at the river, Mr. Bunsen's first-hour class arrived back at school. They carefully labeled their finds and stowed the jars on a shelf in the classroom. The science buffs were excited they would spend the rest of the month carrying out experiments to see what would happen with the mosquito population. One group was allowed to mate and fertilize eggs naturally, and a control group experienced eggs infected with a liquid to alter their DNA. The class filed out. All except one person.

* * * * *

The next day, Marty and Christopher were the first students at the door of the science classroom just before class was scheduled to start. Mr. Bunsen stood outside the classroom, blocking the door.

"I'm sorry to say you can't enter the classroom. Please assemble here. I need to wait for the rest of the class to get here so I can make an announcement," he said.

Marty and Christopher exchanged looks. Marty knew the news was not good. Mr. Bunsen's face had taken on an ashen look and his eyes, normally bright and glistening, registered an unusual dullness. And worse, he had begun to scratch himself everywhere his skin was exposed, his face, neck, and arms.

Soon the rest of the class arrived. There were moans all around as word spread that something was up. Wade was the last to show up. Marty thought he had the look of a Cheshire cat who had just pulled off a milk heist.

"Class, it looks like everyone is here," announced Mr. Bunsen. "What I'm afraid I have to tell you is we won't be entering the classroom today. It seems that some jokester has opened all the jars and set the mosquitoes free."

"What? You've got to be kidding me."

"I can't believe this. We endured more itching for nothing?"

Aisha wrinkled her brow. Marty looked from her to Christopher. He knew by his friend's drooping shoulders that his disappointment matched his own.

"Who would do such a thing?" Wade asked.

The passive bystander would have taken that to be a sincere question, that is, until they realized it came from Wade. Mr. Bunsen and several of the students all looked at Wade and shook their heads.

"Oh, don't you try to pin that on me," Wade cried. "You'll never find any evidence implicating me."

What a peculiar choice of words, Marty thought. Then he realized he could find out who snuck into the classroom and unleashed all those mosquitoes.

At this rate, we won't be able to complete our mosquito research before the semester is done, he worried. There's got to be evidence. That's when he decided right then and there he was the man for the job. He had the equipment. He could start when the dismissal bell rang.

No one noticed the hum of the ever-present drone outside the window of Advanced Science 303.

18
MISSION "SHUT DOWN WADE"

Marty slowly opened the door to his room, and peered inside, half expecting to catch Toni in the act. Though he repeatedly warned her and threatened her with telling their parents, he had the uneasy feeling Toni was still snooping. He couldn't afford to have her wreck his hard-earned spy collection, or even worse, to catch him in the act of bringing one of his creations to life.

He liked the idea of testing his inventions outside the house, but still occasionally tried out something in his room if he suddenly felt inspired or woke up in the middle of the night with an idea. Still, Marty knew that was dangerous. He ran the risk of an invention running rampant throughout the house. So far, that hadn't happened and for that, he was grateful.

Now Marty felt energized. He had a mission. He'd have to give it a name. Mission Shut Down Wade, he decided. And the mission would commence immediately. Marty grabbed his lock picking kit and quickly unlocked the lid of his spy box. He began to pore through the box. Success! He held up his fingerprint kit.

Next, he searched for his spy manual. No luck.

"Now when did I last have that?" Marty mumbled to himself, and scratched his head. I never leave out my spy manual. Maybe I left it in my backpack. I'll get it later.

Minutes later, Marty had laid out on his bed the fingerprint kit, his body wire, lie detector kit, door stop alarm, night goggles, and voice changer. He whipped out his smartphone and searched the school directory for Wade's phone number. He blocked his own number and dialed Wade's number.

"I'd like to speak to Wade," he asked, speaking through his voice changer.

The voice Wade heard was unrecognizable. Marty knew Wade would never figure out who was on the other line. He knew the investment in the device was money well spent.

"Who is this?" Wade demanded to know.

"It's someone who's watching you," Marty warned. "I know what you did and you're not getting away with it."

"What are you talking about?" Wade asked, his voice rising.

"You know darn well what I'm talking about. Actions have consequences and you'll get yours."

Marty listened closely for any concern in Wade's voice.

"I don't know who you think you are, but you're gonna be a dead man when I find out. That's a promise. And I should be able to tell who you are at school tomorrow. By your look of stark terror after you spend the night thinking of how I'm going to break bones when I figure out who you are. And I will," said Wade.

Marty quickly hung up the phone, reminding himself that his voice was totally disguised. Not in a million years would Wade solve the mystery of the caller. He thought about that for a second or two more before reassuring himself of the high ratings of the voice changer. It was Spy Kids approved!

* * * * *

The next day it was Marty who hid in the classroom at the end of the school day. He watched through the closet door peephole as Mr. Bunsen looked at his watch, stretched, and headed for the door, locking it behind him. Marty stood up from his cramped position, and began to stretch his legs. As he reached out to open the closet door, Mr. Bunsen re-entered the classroom, grabbed his jacket, and securely locked the classroom door once again.

Marty then rushed out and got to work, pulling out his spy suitcase. He first took out his gloves and fingerprint kit. He carefully dusted for fingerprints, and used his tape to lift the prints he found. It was difficult to get a good print, since several were overlapping. Nevertheless, he managed to get a small collection. Now all he'd have to do is get Wade's print and see if he had a match.

Next, Marty went over to where Wade normally sat. He took a small, sound-triggered voice recorder and rigged it to the bottom of the seat. If Wade boasted of his deed, Marty would hear of it. And in case Wade held his boasting until he got to the lunchroom, Marty had a plan. He pulled out another voice recorder, disguised as a shiny pen. He was sure Wade wouldn't be able to resist pocketing the pen for himself. All he would need to do is recover it after lunch and play back the lunchtime discussion.

Now, for the night-vision goggles. Marty pulled a granola bar out of his suitcase and settled in. Every good spy or cop knew the perp often returned to the scene of the crime. Marty planned to wait it out for a while to see if Wade returned to the classroom. He was dozing off when he heard a sound. Marty fought his grogginess and snapped to attention. He heard it again. Someone was out there.

Marty tried to quietly stretch his legs and reach for the blinding hand-held flashlight he had brought along. When he heard the noise again, he bolted out of the closet brandishing the flashlight. A scared mouse hurriedly scuttled off. Marty shrank into a seat, dejected. *I guess Christopher won't get the call after all,* he thought.

He wondered if Christopher had been able to sleep. When Marty had told his friend about the plan, Christopher had made him promise to call to come help with the interrogation once Wade was snared. Marty walked over to his suitcase and began to pack it in for the night. The lie detector lay on top.

"Not tonight," he murmured.

* * * * *

As Marty walked away from the school lugging his heavy spy suitcase, he didn't notice the lone car parked at the far end of the school building.

Mr. Bunsen watched someone walk away with his head down. He then got out of his car, walked up to the door, inserted his key, and entered.

He pulled a chair over to the closet door where Marty had hidden, reached above the door, and unlatched a small camera. He smiled, slipped it into his pocket and left the classroom, carefully locking the door behind him.

* * * * *

Back at home, Marty slipped into the house via the back door, and quietly took the stairs two at a time. A door down the hall gently opened. It was Granny, who peered out as Marty's door closed. In his room, Marty placed his spy suitcase on his bed and whipped out his smartphone. He dictated an email message for Christopher.

Operation Shut Down Wade is underway. No

appearance tonight. Just a mouse. But prints in hand. More tomorrow.

Soon after Marty hit send, his phone rang.

"Must you call me each time?" he asked.

"Forget the code. The email is secure. What do you mean just a mouse?"

"Just what I texted," Marty said. "A real mouse. I heard a noise and thought Wade had really returned, but it was just a rodent."

"So back at it tomorrow?" Christopher asked.

"For sure. I've got the prints and the sound-activated voice recorder and voice decoy pen at the ready. Fireworks possible tomorrow," Marty said, yawning.

"Fireworks? Is that code?" Christopher asked, yawning himself.

"Yeah. I mean action. Let's get some sleep," Marty said.

"Agreed. Later."

"Later."

19
INTERNATIONAL GOONS IDENTIFY THEIR TARGET

The drone hovered outside Mr. Bunsen's home. The image was clear and the audio crisp.

The science teacher sat at his kitchen table surrounded by his own video camera and monitor. "It's time we solve this little mystery," said Mr. Bunsen to himself. "There's something strange about Marty, whether his granny wants to admit it or not. I'll get to the bottom of who let those mosquitoes go."

The video playback began.

"What the heck?" Mr. Bunsen yelled.

It was Marty on the tape all right.

He seemed to be rigging the classroom. Mr. Bunsen repeatedly fast forwarded the tape, saw Marty springing out of the closet and chasing after a mouse.

"What is this kid up to?" Mr. Bunsen asked aloud. "I'll have to keep an eye on him for sure."

* * * * *

Marty and Christopher joined a handful of 7th graders who walked over to the Dawg Spot and stuffed their faces with Chicago-style hotdogs. Even though a freeway separated the middle school from the Dawg Spot, there was a convenient tunnel that led to the restaurant, so kids made daily trips to sink their teeth into "The Best Tasting Dawg in the Midwest," or so the commercials said. Large beef franks were loaded with onions, relish, pickles, peppers, and tomatoes, along with mustard and a dash of celery salt.

When the last of their friends had trickled out of the restaurant, Marty and Christopher put their heads together.

"Is it time to put the screws to Wade? Bring out the lie detector kit and the torture apparatus?" Christopher asked, chewing a large bite of hotdog and spraying it all over.

"What torture apparatus? Have you been holding out on me?" Marty asked.

"Just kidding about that last one. Now tell me what you heard from the camera and the video pen?"

"Nada."

"Nada. As in nothing?"

"That's what I said. I can't believe Wade is keeping his lips sealed for a change. What kind of a plan is that? You do something like release a hundred mosquitoes and you don't even take bragging rights," Marty said, shaking his head.

"He's up to something bigger," Christopher said.

"Like what?"

"How should I know?"

Marty polished off the last of his hot dog and stood up. "I'll be right back." He headed toward the restroom. As he looked out the window, he noticed Wade hurriedly making his way to the tunnel.

Marty started to yell for Christopher, then quickly decided to follow Wade. He could explain later.

* * * * *

As Marty crept up behind the other boy, keeping a safe distance, he saw Wade standing in the tunnel looking back and forth between two men. Outside of the one-foot difference in height, they had the same build, dark hair, and rugged complexions. The taller man had a cough that reminded Marty of someone who smoked a couple packs of cigarettes each day.

"We will make it very pleasant for you," the shorter man was saying with a thick accent.

"And enrich your life well beyond what you would ever expect," the Tall Cougher added, also with a strange accent.

Marty saw Wade lean forward. "I thought you were hiring me to snoop on people through new smartphones. I thought the spy book theft and mosquito release were just tests. What are you talking about?"

"We know your specialty," the smaller man said. Wade caught a whiff of the worst breath he had ever smelled. He had to stop himself from grabbing his nose. He didn't want to offend these men until he heard what they wanted from him.

"Specialty?" Wade asked.

"We show you," the Tall Cougher said.

He produced the most compact Drone Marty had ever seen. It was silver and black with blinking green and yellow lights. The man pushed a button, causing a holographic image to pop up. It was Wade on the first day of their Advanced Science class, skipping from table to table.

Marty had to clamp his hands over his mouth when he saw Wade's excited movements. He yearned to move closer but knew he had to stay out of sight if he was going to find out what Wade was up to.

The three huddled closer together, preventing Marty from hearing what was being said. Again, he debated moving up. He stifled a sneeze. Something told him the two men were hard cases. Wade could hang out with them if he wanted to, but Marty wasn't taking any chances. He thought he had seen that drone before. What were those guys doing with it and what did this have to do with Wade?

* * * * *

Wade shook hands with the two goons, promising to be in touch.

"Do I need a number for you guys?" he asked.

"We will contact you," Tall Cougher said, promptly launching into a coughing fit.

"You really need to give up the smokes," said the smaller man.

"And you need the extra-strength mouthwash, Bad Breath."

Minutes later, Marty watched Wade walked out of the tunnel with a definite strut in his step, a lightness. A passive bystander might describe it as the confident stride of someone who had just been told he held the winning lottery number, or a kid finally gifted with the puppy of his dreams.

Wade was flying high, feeling as if he owned the world. He had begun to think of himself as much more than just your everyday kid. He was a man on a mission. He had been chosen, and given an assignment that, if handled successfully, would make him a rich man. Wade would become the go-to person for all of his classmates, and for students all over the U.S., even those who had never met him.

In fact, he could become legendary. Zuckerman, who created Facebook with its two billion users worldwide, and the late great Steve Jobs, the inventor of the Mac, iPhone, iPod and iPad, who revolutionized the way people communicate, would be nothing next to him.

Why, he would live in the mansion of his choice, in the city or country he wanted, own a Ferrari and a fleet of fast, expensive cars. He'd have a Sweet Sixteen party on MTV every weekend, and would jet in hip-hoppers and rock and rollers, paying their exorbitant fees, and putting them up in lavish resorts and hotels. He'd fly his favorite Chicago-style hotdog and pizza into whichever city he happened to be laying his head that week.

Wade suddenly cut short his dream of excesses in his newly imagined life. *Wait a minute*, he thought. *If I possess this power, and I do, I saw what I could do before my own eyes, where did this power come from? Was it given to me? Inherited? Whoa, maybe my parents have it too!*

Wade quickly walked home. When he entered the family room, his mom sat there watching her favorite afternoon talk show.

"Hi, Wade," she said, barely looking up.

"Hi, Mom. Hey, did…" he began.

"Did you say something? If you are going to ask to go out, let me tell you a thing or two. First, you're late. You were told to come right home and get started on the laundry you didn't do this weekend. Secondly..."

Wade didn't wait to hear the rest. He bounded up the stairs to his room two at a time, with a new idea.

His mom passively dropped the one-sided conversation, and turned back to her television show.

Wade faced his bedroom door. He placed his five fingers on the Biometric Scanner Room Guard. The device kept anyone but him and his fingerprints out of his bedroom and clearly spelled out "off limits."

His parents had initially given him grief but neither was interested enough in anything he did to really insist on its removal. For his mom, it spared her the sight of her only son's messy room. His dad was so busy running his failing low-grade restaurant that he wasn't home for more than an hour or two at a time, anyway. Awake, that is. So, Wade was pretty much left to his own devices.

This afternoon, that served him well. He scanned himself in, and quickly slammed the door behind him, barely netting a glance upstairs from his mom. He quickly pulled out a dictionary and several minutes later, had memorized its entire contents. Next, he grabbed a chemistry textbook. The goons were right. Wade had always had this ability. He could always ace whatever quiz or test he took by spending just a few minutes studying.

Maybe that's why I get into so much trouble, he thought. *I mess with folks to keep myself from getting bored.*

Wade glanced at his watch, and realized it was dawn. It's funny how patiently he could read when he realized he would be rewarded with a successful mission and riches beyond his imagination.

His stomach growled. He headed downstairs in the dark to see if his mom had even bothered to prepare any dinner. The refrigerator held a stinky casserole, condiments, beer, and Coca-Cola. And just-bought ingredients for her book club dinner.

Wade spotted an open cookbook. He smiled and in a flurry, began reading, mixing, and cooking. Once the lasagna and chicken cacciatore were prepared, he grabbed the cookbook again, memorized the next recipe, and started in on sausage stuffing.

A couple of hours later, Wade sat gorging on the lasagna, chicken cacciatore, stuffing, yams, green beans, and strawberry cheesecake. He heard his alarm clock go off in his bedroom. The kitchen door slowly swung open. His bleary-eyed mom appeared, her hair in curlers, and clutching closed her old, tattered blue robe. She stared at him, speechless.

"Mom, come on in!" Wade yelled. "I've learned to cook! Have some dinner!"

His mom promptly fainted.

20
GRANNY SCHOOLS MARTY
ON HIS SUPER POWERS

Marty, Aisha, and Christopher squealed as they raced their bumper cars at the indoor track. They jostled against each other, cutting off the closest car, and bumping each other to gain advantage. After a couple of rounds, they saw Wade in line. He grabbed a car and tore down the track after them, banging into Marty.

"There you go. There's no getting around me now!" Wade yelled. Marty easily skirted by him and raced ahead. After a few minutes of Wade hungrily banging and jostling all three, Marty began to get a bit upset. Aisha seemed to be getting the worse of it.

"Wade, stop it! We were having a great time until you came along to spoil it!" Aisha yelled.

"Isn't that too bad? It's a free country, you know. I paid my money just like everyone else. Besides, the bumper car is also called a 'dodgem,' a flat electric car used to...."

"Great. Good to know, Wade," Christopher said.

"I've got another one for you. Who invented the bumper car and why did he think it was a good idea to place bumpers on the car?" Wade asked.

"Why this sudden interest in the history of bumper cars?" Marty asked Wade. "Next you'll be reciting the history of the Ferris wheel."

"Oh, I can tell you about that…" Wade began.

"Can it!" Marty yelled. "Come on, guys, let's move on." Marty's friends agreed and all three began to maneuver to the drop-off point.

"Hey! We're just getting started!" Wade yelled, and with that, he ferociously yelled and bumped Aisha, causing her to chomp down on her lip, drawing blood. The blood dribbled down her chin.

"Look what you've done," she cried.

A change came over Marty's face. He saw the blood and lost track of what happened next. It wasn't until Christopher later recounted the events that Marty was able to recall all of his actions.

Marty whipped out his smartphone and imagined ferrets. Suddenly, racing ferrets materialized and began swarming over Wade's head. Marty nodded. The ferrets seemed to pounce all at once, biting Wade and sending him running from the car.

Onlookers couldn't figure out why the boy was running and screaming headed for the track's exit doors. Then they noticed the crazed ferrets, seeming to have a taste for the blood of a sole victim. When the bumper car operator went to check on him minutes later, he found a frantically scratching Wade, with large welts developing all over his body.

"I'm going to want you to call 911," he yelled over his shoulder at a co-worker.

At that moment, Marty, Aisha, and Christopher walked by Wade and his scratching fit. The ferrets were fleeing the park. Marty's smug smile said it all. In seconds, the ferrets evaporated.

* * * * *

The three ended up in Marty's backyard. Granny opened a window.

"Dinner will be ready in just a few minutes," she yelled. She jumped at the loud laughter.

"And he'll never forget the crazed ferrets at the track. Here's my imitation of Wade," Marty said. He frantically ran throughout the yard, waving his arms, fending off pretend invaders. "Guess the call for paramedics will teach him a lesson he won't soon forget."

"Man, that was awesome. You outdid yourself this time!" Christopher laughed, slapping Marty on the back.

Aisha laughed along. "That was a funny sight. Hey, where did the ferrets come from?"

Granny stuck her head out of the window. "Marty, can you come in for a minute, please?"

"In a few minutes, Granny. I won't be long," Marty shouted.

"Let me rephrase that," Granny said. "I need you right now."

Something in her voice told Marty the summons was real. He said goodnight to his friends and went inside. Granny stood in the kitchen with her arms folded.

"Yeah, Granny?"

"What was that you were talking to your friends about?"

"Oh, that was nothing."

"Oh, it was something all right. I need you to tell me the story. And start from the beginning."

Marty wondered if Granny was on to his powers. He should have felt afraid to reveal his secret, but a part of him felt a huge sense of relief. It was time he shared what he had been grappling with for some time now. Granny was always there for him. Sure, her plain talk sometimes spooked him.

When he was younger, she didn't hesitate to spank him when he disobeyed. But when he grew old enough to understand, he felt it was all out of love.

He took a deep breath and plunged right in. "I've been testing out these powers for some time. I am able to use my smartphone to pull up a drawing app, focus on it, and get what I want to…well, it comes to life," Marty hurriedly added. "It lasts for just a while."

"I see," Granny said.

The fact that she didn't express surprise or horror calmed Marty with a certainty he hadn't felt before. In that moment, he felt as close to his grandmother as he had ever felt. She reached over, pulled him to her, and wrapped her arms around him.

"You've got it. You've got the power. You're not the only one, so let's talk about what it is. It's a gift," Granny said.

Marty pulled away, his eyes filled with the countless questions he now had.

Granny smiled, "It's going to take a while to answer all your questions. It was the same way for me."

Marty's mouth fell open in surprise.

"Yep, that's right. My powers were revealed to me when I was just a little older than you. They're different than yours. And I'll tell you all about them sometime. For now, let's focus on you," she said.

Marty nodded, tears filling his eyes.

He followed Granny into the family room, where they sat down in comfortable recliners.

"You started with the Etch-A-Sketch. I could tell you were fascinated with the ability to turn shapes into animals, buildings, or faces," Granny stared into space. "No, I began to wonder much earlier than that. There was a time when I was babysitting for you. I never figured out how you managed to get the rattle off the shelf from your spot on the floor. You were just a baby."

"Are you saying I've had this ability since I was a baby?" Marty asked.

"I wasn't sure if your powers were something you would grow out of. You became fascinated with spy gadgets. I didn't see any more evidence of it over the years," Granny said, placing her hand in Marty's.

"That explains a lot," Marty said. "I always felt like a freak. Why was I seeing things move when I had just drawn them on paper or on my Etch-A-Sketch? They only lasted a minute, so I just thought it was my imagination."

"Many in the Order of Hannibal have that experience. You see, you don't yet have all the tools. I want you to promise me. Promise me you will not use your superpowers until I say you're ready."

Marty's heart was racing. He would have sworn his granny had stopped talking, but her lips were still moving. *Superpowers? Me? Marty?*

Granny knew what her grandson was feeling. Like Spiderman and all the other superheroes before him, herself included, he just didn't fully understand what he had.

* * * * *

The sky darkened as they talked. His mom and dad returned home with Toni. Granny spoke to them briefly before returning to Marty. By the time he went to bed that evening, he felt liberated and fully at peace for the first time since he became aware of his powers.

Granny slept fitfully. She now knew the powers Marty possessed and what lie ahead. The details were uncertain. What she knew for sure was he would be tested. Opposition always arose to challenge great power. She feared for her grandson.

21
AISHA TESTS NIGHT GOGGLES

Marty woke up the next day jazzed. It was a Sunday so he wouldn't have to worry about school. His conversation with Granny had led to an idea. He grabbed his wallet and headed out the door. His dad stopped him.

"Hey, where are you going in such a big hurry?"

"Oh, hi, Dad. No place special. I wanted to take my allowance and, er … pick up a few automotive magazines. You know, at Morrey's," Marty stammered.

"A boy and his cars. I became interested in cars when I was about your age. It's a few years before you can drive, but that doesn't stop one from dreaming, does it?" he teased.

"You're right about that."

"Maybe I can go with you. We haven't had much man time since my work schedule got crazy," his dad said.

Marty's mom rounded the corner with Toni in tow. "Not so fast, Larry. You were going to get started on that slow-draining faucet, remember? In fact, Marty can give you a hand with that."

"Oh, boy. My honey-do list just exploded," his dad said. "You know what, Marty? Go ahead. I've got a couple other chores I want you to do this afternoon. I can get started on the faucet myself."

Thanks, Dad!" Marty yelled, bursting out the door before his mom could put in a veto.

"I want to go," he heard Toni whine as the door slammed behind him. "I wonder if he has powers stuff to do." She spoke the latter so softly no one heard her.

"What fire was he headed to?" Marty's mom wanted to know.

"Something about going to Morrey's to check out the car magazines," Larry said.

"Oh, boy, now that's one stage I'm not quite ready for. The Marty-on-the-street-with-a-driver's-license stage."

"Mom, maybe Marty can drive me and my friends to the movies," Toni suggested helpfully.

"Baby, it will be a few years before Marty can drive. But I'm sure if you ask when he gets back, he'll save a spot for you," mom said with a glint in her eye.

Marty's dad responded with his deep booming laugh.

Granny walked down the stairs rubbing her eyes. It was clear she hadn't slept much at all.

* * * * *

Mr. Bunsen's 7th grade classroom was back in session on Monday morning. An order of fresh mosquitoes had arrived. Rumor had it he had paid for them out of his own pocket. Nothing was going to stop this semester's research. The students buzzed with excitement as they prepared to begin their delayed laboratory experiments.

Marty and Aisha shared a few pointed glances as they worked through the exercises Mr. Bunsen had designed.

Mr. Bunsen had shifted groups based on their grasp of the CRISPR-Cas9 gene-editing technology. Marty, Christopher, Aisha, and Wade were now on the same team. Marty wasn't too happy about that.

Neither were the others. Yet, Wade's focus on the work was undeniable.

The group of four huddled over a microscope. They took turns peering in. Marty felt better about the upcoming test.

* * * * *

As they had planned, Aisha joined him outside the school when the bell rang. They walked to Marty's house, talking about their science project and the latest spy gadgets on the Spy Museum website.

Marty was relieved to see no one was home yet. He bounded up the stairs to his room, with Aisha closely on his heels.

Marty quickly went to work opening his spy box.

"Are you sure you're ready for this?" he asked.

"Come on. I can take it," Aisha said.

With a flourish, Marty flung open the box, and began to pick out goodies for closer inspection. Aisha moved her head closer, straining to get a good look at the spy box contents.

"I didn't think girls went in for this kind of thing," admitted Marty.

"What's that supposed to mean?" Aisha asked, pouting.

"No offense! I mean..."

"You may want to stop while you're ahead, Marty Hayes. If you're such a fan of the Spy Museum, then I know you've heard of Mata Hari and Josephine Baker. I see that you know Harriet Tubman." She motioned to his wall poster.

"You know that Harriet Tubman was also a spy? How do you know all this?"

"How else? I visited the Spy Museum with my family last summer. Now, let me have a look at the night goggles."

Marty helped Aisha place the goggles onto her head and showed her how to operate them as he dimmed the lights in the room.

"As I work the lights, let me know if things are getting clearer," Marty said.

"Oh, I see, yes, I can see better. Are you making it darker now?"

Marty played with the dim switches, while Aisha took the goggles on and off.

"Now walk around and see if you can avoid bumping into things."

Aisha did as Marty instructed. Chez Vous suddenly ran into the room, and started jumping up and down, begging for attention.

"Not now. Not now. Sorry Aisha, let me get the dog out of here," said Marty, scooping Chez Vous up into his arms. "Keep practicing. I'll be right back."

Marty headed for the door. The minute he walked out, Aisha dropped the night goggles onto a table. She placed her hands over her eyes, then slowly lowered them. She repeated the exercise Marty had shown her, only using her own eyes in the pitch-black darkness.

She walked backwards around the room, successfully navigating each piece of furniture and each obstruction without a single bump. By the time Marty returned, Aisha had convinced herself. She had the ability to use her night-vision powers with her own eyes, even in totally unfamiliar settings.

Aisha and Marty spent a few more minutes going through his spy box. Finally, he stood up and closed the lid.

"It's a school night. I'd better get you home," Marty said.

"Ok. I don't want to give my parents any excuse for limiting our time studying. The science test is right around the corner."

"Don't I know? Let's go," Marty said, leading the way.

* * * * *

After Aisha arrived home, she nibbled at her dinner, asked to be excused, and said goodnight to her parents. Back in her room, she walked over to her dresser and opened her jewelry box. She pulled out a photo of her grandma wearing a medal, nearly identical to the one Marty's Granny owned. Aisha uncovered the medal and fingered it.

"Thanks, Grandma Janet. I think I'm ready."

22
GRANNY GOES DOWN

The next afternoon, Marty burst through the front door eager to share the good news of his 'A' on his science test. He had already celebrated with Christopher and Aisha on their trio of As. Wade had taken off with a weird expression immediately after getting his grade.

"Hey! Anybody home?" Marty yelled.

He heard Chez Vous bark in her pen in the first-floor laundry room. He went to let her out. "Hello, anybody?"

Marty hurriedly decided to take Chez Vous out for a quick walk so he could take care of his business. In his haste, he forgot to grab a plastic bag to dispose of any poop. They walked for a few feet to the nearest stop sign. Like clockwork. Chez Vous stopped to sniff. Another few feet—sniff, sniff. *Dang,* Marty thought. Dogs truly have a misplaced sense of smell. They can't even go for a decent walk without stopping every foot or so. So much for exercise.

Suddenly, Chez Vous squatted down. *There he goes,* Marty thought. *And me without a bag.* After Chez Vous finished his business, Marty sheepishly looked around. No one in sight. He took off running, pulling the dog after him.

"He's fleeing the scene! He's fleeing the scene!" he thought. Marty started laughing, with Chez Vous excitedly running with him.

Soon, they were back home. The neighbors were none the wiser.

His dad appeared. "Marty, there you are. I got a call from your mom. We have to go to the hospital."

The hospital?" Marty asked. "Why?"

"It's Granny. She's been pretty exhausted these last few days. And when your mom got home, she found her unconscious. Good thing Toni wasn't home to see the commotion. I just dropped Toni off next door. Let's get going."

Marty and his dad hurried out to the car.

* * * * *

When they arrived at the hospital, Marty took a deep breath. His dad didn't seem to know much about how Granny was doing. But Dad was chewing his bottom lip like he did when he was worried, so

Marty was on edge. He didn't know what he'd do without his granny. He visualized her in happier times and wished his powers allowed him to cure people. *I'd give up everything if it saved Granny,* he thought.

They quickly found the room they were looking for, and entered to find his mom stroking Granny's hand. Mrs. Hayes jumped up and hugged her husband, followed by Marty. His mom touched Marty's hair.

"She's doing better. She asked for you," she said.

"Has the doctor seen her since she was brought to her room?" Marty's dad asked.

"Yeah. He said...," she stopped, and looked at Marty's worried face. "Why don't we talk outside and give Marty a chance to spend a few minutes alone?"

They walked out leaving Marty with his beloved granny. She reached for Marty's hand.

"Now don't you go creasing your face up with those worry lines. What did I tell you about growing up too fast? I'm doing much better. I knew you had it in you to ace that science test. All that mosquito studying should mean zero bites for me next summer."

"Oh, Granny," Marty said, flooding with relief. At least, she hadn't lost her sense of humor.

She closed her eyes as if the effort to talk had worn her out. Marty was keenly attuned to her feelings and felt as if his own chest hurt. They sat in silence for a while until his parents returned. Marty searched their faces for answers. He hated when they tried to shield him from "grown-up" talk. He was worried now that they wouldn't tell him the full story about Granny's condition for fear of spooking him.

Marty's mom looked at him. She could see the depths of his concern.

"It's all my fault!" he blurted.

His mom and dad exchanged glances. "What are you talking about? This isn't anyone's fault," his mom said. "Granny just hadn't been taking very good care of herself. She's just suffering from dehydration and her blood pressure is low."

"It's more than that!" Marty said, growing more agitated. "We talked about both of us having the power."

A strange look came over Marty's mom's face. He had the feeling she knew exactly what he meant without Marty needing to say another word.

23
MARTY RECEIVES THE
ORDER OF HANNIBAL MEDAL

In the following days, Marty sensed that his mom was about to say something more to him about "the powers," but she never did. Then one day, as he was surfing the Internet for new spy gadgets, she knocked on his door.

"Hi," she said. "Can I come in for a minute?"

"Sure, Mom," Marty said, peeling his eyes from the computer screen.

His mom sat on the edge of his bed. "I know it's been tough for you with Granny's sickness. I thought of something that will make you feel a lot better."

"What's that?" Marty asked. She now had his full attention.

"Well, I have an assignment in Washington, D.C. I thought maybe you'd like to go."

"Oh, yeah!" Marty screamed, throwing his arms around her neck. "Wait until I tell Granny!"

* * * * *

Later that day, Marty joined Granny at the hospital, eager to tell her all about his upcoming trip to Washington D.C. and the International Spy Museum. His mom left the hospital room to get them both a soda.

"The last time I visited, they had a lot of stuff in the store they didn't sell online," Marty gushed. "I can't wait to see what they have. I'm taking my money that I've got saved up. Mom says I can spend as much as I want. I'll get you something, too, Granny."

"Oh, don't you worry about your old granny. It does me good to see you so happy," Granny said.

Suddenly her mood grew somber. "Marty, I need to tell you something. Not everyone is as they seem. There is evil in the world. Evil lives when good men do nothing. And with our gifts, we're called upon to use it when it will make a difference. With your powers, I couldn't believe what I was seeing. They started when you were so young. That's extraordinary. That says to me what you've got is truly special."

"What about Mom and Dad. Do they know?"

"They know a little about me. You've heard a little about my work during the Civil Rights movement. That's when I came into my powers. And I put them to good use," Granny said.

Marty's eyes widened. "You talk about Dr. Martin Luther King and the Montgomery bus boycott."

"Dr. King worked hard to make sure people treated each other as equals, and not like too many people, based on the color of their skin. I made sure the few busses that were ignoring the boycott Dr. King supported to stop discrimination on busses, and in society, hit a few speedbumps along the way," Granny grinned. "They never did find out why those busses were lurching so on those smooth streets."

"And your photo with the little girl who integrated the school in New Orleans?"

"Ruby Bridges was a brave little girl. My parents wouldn't let me go to that all-white school. But Ruby's parents had a rare breed of brave. I skipped school that day. I was able to help out a bit. It didn't take me long to spot the boy with the BB gun. When he fell face down on that rippling concrete, that was the end of that gun. It broke into pieces," Granny said with a slight smile.

Marty fell silent, trying to absorb all Granny was telling him. His mom would return in minutes, so he knew he needed to ask all he could in the little time he had left.

"Why do my animals and creations seem to have a short lifespan?" Marty asked.

"You don't have the Order medal," Granny said, sighing deeply. "Give me my bag over there."

Marty stared at Granny, and then followed her finger to the closet where he found a black leather overnight bag. As if in a trance, he picked it up and brought it to Granny's bedside. She unzipped the bag, and pulled out the medal. Marty recognized it immediately. It was the same medal Granny and his granddad wore in the photo.

"This medal is only worn by members of the Order of Hannibal. Only another member can pass it on to the next generation. You'll find that it gives your actions clarity and greater control. In your case, you'll be able to lengthen the lifespan of what you create. Carry this on you at all times. Don't lose it," Granny advised, handing the medal over to Marty.

As Marty started to take a closer look at the medal, his mom entered the room carrying two sodas. Granny gave him a stern look. He knew that meant their conversation was private. Marty slipped the medal into his pocket before his mom noticed.

"Here you go," she said brightly, setting her mother's soda on her bedside tray.

She handed the second soda to Marty. It was Dr. Pepper, his favorite. He downed it in a few gulps, fingering the medal in his pocket.

"Well, someone's awfully thirsty," Mom said. She looked at Granny who smiled and closed her eyes.

"Mom, are you all right?" she asked.

"I could use a little nap," she answered. Marty and Mom said their goodbyes. Marty thought Granny squeezed him a little tighter than usual when he wrapped his arms around her to say goodbye.

24

JETTING OFF TO THE NATION'S CAPITAL

Toni pouted during much of the ride to the airport. She brightened as they got closer once she noticed large planes flying overhead.

"Where are all those people going?" she asked.

Marty smiled. He was sure that in her 6-year-old mind everyone was headed to an exotic spot, and to her, that would mean a trip to Disneyland, like the one they had taken last year.

Marty's dad followed signs to the passenger unloading area. Marty fingered his new medal before jumping out of the car, clutching his overnight bag. His mom followed suit, and beckoned to Toni to join her curbside. As Marty's dad hopped out to pull their suitcases out of the car's trunk, his mom leaned down and cradled Toni in her arms.

"Now, Mommy wants you to be a big girl for Dad until we get back. We'll bring you a nice treat."

"Ok, Mommy. I will. But I want to go with you and Marty to the Spy Museum. It's my favorit-est place too, next to Disneyland."

"Disneyland? Did someone say Disneyland?" Marty's mom reached into her pocket and pulled out a large stuffed lion like the one in *The Lion King*, Toni's favorite musical.

"*The Lion King!*" Toni shouted, clutching the stuffed animal to her chest. With his dad and mom exchanging smiles, Marty fingered his medal. He looked on with surprise as the lion began to come alive. Toni tightly clutched the animal now writhing in her grasp. Instinctively, Marty rubbed the medal frantically. The lion slowly withered before his eyes and regained its dormant state.

"The Lion King moves!" Toni cried.

But Mom and Dad were too busy handling luggage to notice. Marty looked toward the sky, breathed a sigh of relief and vowed to be more careful. Granny hadn't finished telling him the whole story of his powers. There was a lot he still needed to figure out for himself.

* * * * *

As they walked into the airport, Marty was a bit distracted. He thought of Granny and was grateful she had begun to improve following their last visit. It was almost as if a burden had been lifted.

It was a great surprise when his mom told him he would get to visit the International Spy Museum.

"There they are!" Mrs. Hayes said.

"Who?" Marty asked. Then he saw him. Walking toward them with a huge grin on his face was Christopher, closely followed by his mom.

"Surprise!" Christopher yelled. "You didn't think I was going to let you go to the Spy Museum without me, did you?"

The teens threw their arms around each other. "Oh, Mom, you are the best!" Marty cried. His mom's heart melted. It was the happiest she had seen him since Granny became ill.

"Thank Mrs. Greene. It was her idea to allow Christopher to come along to keep you company," Mom said.

"Thanks, Mrs. Greene."

"A million thanks, Mom," Christopher said, throwing his arms around his own mother's neck.

"You just make sure you behave. You're going to the Spy Museum, but don't forget that this is a working trip for Mrs. Hayes, so don't give her a headache," Christopher's mom advised.

"Josephine, I'm sure the boys won't be any trouble. I'm just happy Chris could come along," Marty's mom said.

The foursome headed to the check-in counter. Before long, Mrs. Greene was waving goodbye from the security checkpoint.

* * * * *

Christopher and Marty sat peering out the window. With a smile, Marty's mom, in the aisle seat, pulled out her folder on Washington, D.C. As the plane lifted off, she said aloud a little prayer for a safe trip and for Granny's speedy recovery.

25
MARTY AND CHRISTOPHER ARE IN FOR A SURPRISE

The plane descended at Reagan National Airport. Marty and Christopher could barely contain their joy. Nearby passengers smiled listening to the two bright kids excitedly chat about all they would do when they arrived at the International Spy Museum.

Before they knew it, the boys were speeding in a taxi to their hotel.

"First stop, the rooftop pool," Mrs. Hayes announced.

"Yay!" the boys yelled in unison.

* * * * *

The Pinckney Hotel was a favorite of Mrs. Hayes whenever she stayed in Washington D.C. It was conveniently located and had a restaurant owned by a former personal chef to the stars! Of course, the rooftop pool with its open-air design was a treat. On previous writing trips, Mrs. Hayes had typed her travel articles poolside on her laptop, enjoying the occasional natural breeze, much preferred to a stuffy business office or hotel room.

Making her living as a travel writer since way before Marty was born, she most enjoyed traveling to new places and sharing her finds with adventurers like herself. On this trip, she was looking forward to delighting Marty with one last surprise, while getting her own work done.

They were scarcely at poolside before she announced. "Marty and Christopher, I have another surprise for you."

The boys looked at her eagerly. "Bring it on, bring it on," Marty cried.

"Drum roll, please," Mrs. Hayes said.

The boys obliged.

"I didn't think a trip of just a couple of hours to the Spy Museum would be enough. So, I did some research and found they are offering an overnight spy excursion while we're in town. You boys are going tonight!"

"Mom, you're kidding!?"

"Mrs. Hayes, I love you!" Christopher screamed.

"I knew you'd love it. I'll drop you off at 8 tonight and will pick you up at 10 tomorrow morning."

"Fourteen whole hours!" Marty quickly deduced.

"That's right," his mom said.

"This calls for a celebratory dip," Marty said as he ran to the edge of the pool and jumped in.

"Right behind you!" Christopher called as he pulled his legs into a cannonball.

"Marco!" Marty yelled.

"Polo!" Christopher screamed, creating a huge splash.

Mrs. Hayes threw her wrap aside and joined the boys. She had to struggle to stay above water as they leaped on her and smothered her with hugs and kisses.

While they enjoyed frolicking in the water, another plane was landing at Reagan National Airport. Peering out the window was none other than Wade, the school bully, seated alongside the two men who had earlier approached him.

"So, are we here?" he asked.

"In a few hours, you'll be at the Spy Museum," Tall Cougher answered.

"We'll all be," harrumphed Bad Breath. "And the goods had better be there."

26

LOOK WHO'S ATTENDING THE SPY MUSEUM OVERNIGHT EVENT

The group checking into the Spy Museum was made up of ages ranging from 9 to 13. The kids represented all nationalities and were dressed in various colorful outfits, some donning the outfits of well-known spies, such as James Bond, Mata Hari, and one of Marty's favorites, Josephine Baker.

The younger ones were already in pajamas. In addition to their overnight bags, many clutched spy cases with their names. One kid had already whipped open his case, against his mom's protests, and begun dusting the front door for fingerprints.

Amateur, Marty thought. *With all the people passing through these doors, there won't be a clear print anywhere on the premises.*

At that moment, a tall, thin, bespectacled man with a ruddy complexion walked up to the front doors in full spy regalia.

"Excuse me sir, can I help you?" the door attendant asked.

"Is this the entrance for the overnight spy festivities?" the man eagerly asked.

"Yes. It is. Do you have a kid you'd like to register?"

"No kid," the man answered. "I'd like to attend."

The attendant choked back a smile, and cleared his throat. It wasn't unusual for someone beyond the age limit of 13 to try to get in, but this was pushing all boundaries. "I'm sorry sir, no adults are allowed. Regulations, you know."

The man's face fell. "But, I'm willing to pay."

"Sir, like I said, it's against the rules. No adults are allowed in unless they're on staff. Otherwise, it's a wrap."

A minute or two later, Marty saw the attendant escorting the tall man to the sidewalk. The man left in a huff.

When he got a couple of blocks away, he whipped out a smartphone. "They're entering now. No adults except the few staffers. Send him in."

The number of kids going into the museum had swelled, so they were being split into two groups at the entryway and sent down two different pathways to get in. Marty and Christopher were ushered into one group.

Wade followed shortly and was sent with the other group. The strut Wade had leaving the tunnel outside The Dawg Spot was in full effect. Wade now walked with an electric energy.

* * * * *

Once inside, Marty and Christopher slapped each other on the shoulder. The museum would be all theirs for the next several hours! They followed directions to check in their overnight bags and take out whatever they wanted to carry for the first spy mission. Marty eagerly checked the contents of his spy bag, making sure he had everything he needed. Everything but his spy manual.

Christopher had stuffed his gear into a backpack, so he went through the same checking process.

Between them, they had nearly everything a spy would need for the most elaborate mission. An adult spy leader had been assigned to their group. Marty guessed he was in his early 20s. He introduced himself as Ian.

Ian was dressed all in black, topped by a fedora and trench coat. He opened his coat later to reveal an impressive array of spy gadgets. Marty and Christopher nodded in satisfaction. Rounding out their team were twins, Gregory and Gina. They each wore an overstuffed backpack and seemed excited to meet Marty and Christopher.

"Did you see the kid dusting for prints at the entrance?" Gregory asked.

"Remedial sleuth," Gina said.

"That's what I call a perfect waste of dusting powder. There's no way he can get a usable print for an investigation," Christopher agreed.

"Ok, spies, let's start our first mission," Ian said.

The four young people gathered around Ian to get their mission details. They were given a map of the Spy Museum, which illustrated areas marked by trip wire and those shut off for the overnight expedition.

Marty and Christopher set off together. Marty wondered if some overzealous kid had previously wandered into areas that caused someone a lot of trouble. Oh, well, they had all night to get into the good stuff he was sure was coming.

Christopher stopped for a moment to tie his shoelace. While Marty waited, he looked around.

"No, it can't be," he said aloud.

"Can't be, what?" Christopher asked.

"Not what. Who? And the who appears to be Wade from school."

Christopher jumped up. "You're crazy! Why would Wade be at the Spy Museum?"

"I don't know," Marty said as if from a distance. "But, we need to find out."

Marty felt his heart pump a bit faster. He was quite annoyed that Wade had materialized out of thin air.

"I'm not about to let him spoil our good time. Not here at the museum," Marty said. He quickly walked to the area where he had last spotted Wade. Christopher was on Marty's heels.

It seemed the quicker they moved, the more elusive Wade became.

"He's made us!" Marty cried, as Wade began to run. Marty and Christopher took up the chase, determined to stop Wade and find out why he was in Washington, D.C. *It's not even a school break,* Marty thought. *Why, we wouldn't even be here if not for Mom's travel writing assignment. Why the heck is he here?*

"Wade!" Marty yelled.

After a few minutes of ducking around corners and checking various dark corners, Christopher was getting winded.

"I'll get him," Marty called. He ran ahead, leaving Christopher leaning against a lamppost. The next corner he turned, he came face to face with Wade, nearly bumping into him.

"What the heck do you think you're doing?" Wade demanded.

"Having a great time. That is, until you showed up," Marty scowled.

"Listen, don't you even think about messing this up for me," Wade said, wagging his finger in Marty's face.

"Ha! I should be saying the same to you. It usually works the other way around, doesn't it?

Everyone's having a fine time, that is, until...you show up."

"All I gotta say is I've got a lot on the line here. And the best thing you can do is stay...out...of...my...way," Wade said, stabbing a finger in Marty's chest with each word. He turned and shot down an aisle, quickly moving out of sight.

Marty breathed a deep sigh and closely surveyed his surroundings for the first time. "Where the heck am I?"

As he reached for his smartphone app of the museum, Marty heard voices. It was the team leader Ian and Christopher.

"Hey!" he called.

Ian turned sharply and headed straight toward him. He jerked Marty by the arm. "You can't take off like that. The mission was to be completed in one hour. If it goes much beyond that, you're presumed to be missing. And we have to alert security."

"Did you?" Marty asked. "And keep your hands to yourself."

"You were just under the hour. He was about to," said Christopher.

"You're lucky. But, I'll be keeping a close eye on you," Ian warned. "Follow me."

Christopher and Marty followed closely on Ian's heels, whispering back and forth.

"Did you catch him?" Christopher asked.

"I did and it wasn't pretty. It's bad enough that he's here, but he was clearly up to something," Marty said.

The teens walked in silence. Soon Ian had steered them back to their group where Gregory and Gina were reviewing their next mission.

"This is going to be so cool!" Gina said. "It's our first time here. I'm so excited we were able to do the overnight."

"I intend to be the grand prize winner. It says right here, 'based on fulfillment of the assigned missions'..." Gregory read.

"Does it say what the prize is?" Christopher interrupted, jumping up and down.

"A behind-the-scenes tour, a $500 spy gift card, a spy wardrobe..." Gregory said.

"A lifetime membership to get in free to the Museum, and an interview for the Spy Museum Newsletter..." Gina finished.

"Wow! Who wouldn't want all that? So let's get to our mission. We don't want to give up our chance for the big prizes," Marty suggested.

All four heads nodded. Marty glanced at their team leader, Ian, who stood off to the side checking his smartphone. Clearly, he was more interested in his personal affairs than tending to the eager spy sleuths under his care. *That works just fine*, Marty thought as he watched Ian. *I have a feeling I'm going to need some space in this museum. Ian constantly underfoot is the last thing I need.*

27
MARTY'S ON WADE'S TRAIL

Marty realized he would need to tap into everything he knew about spying to outmaneuver Wade. He was used to Wade, the bully, the prankster who drew his fun from tripping up others, and outwitting them for his own pleasure. But this new Wade was different.

Marty's group was off on its second mission. Wade had no idea Marty had managed to plant a tracking device on him. The clear microchip was devised with a special adhesive to cling to whatever surface it was slapped on.

Marty again opened the app distributed at the beginning of the evening. The areas of the museum open for the spy kids overnight event were clearly marked. *Of course.* His intel was clearly showing Wade in an unauthorized area.

Marty looked at the spy group leader. As usual, Ian was on his phone, this time pleading with his girlfriend to give him another chance.

"Baby, please," he said. "This time it will be different."

Marty thought it a shame only half the conversation could be heard. This one was a doozy.

"I know I've said it before, but this time I mean it...No, I'm not saying I didn't mean it before. I know now how much you mean to me and I want to be with just you...No, no, yes, I mean, no, I won't stray...hold on."

Gina was asking a question. The spy leader searched his pockets and remembered he had left the spy bag for this mission behind.

"I'll be right back," Ian told the group, walking back in the direction from which they had just come. Gina and Gregory looked at each other.

"I've always wanted to just explore this place. Who knew we were going to have to spend the entire night with an escort?" Gina sighed.

Gregory broke out into a wide grin. "Here's our chance. Hey, I don't believe Ian will tell on us. It's four against one. The guy is too broken-hearted about his girlfriend to pay attention to us anyway. I say we do him a favor."

"You don't have to tell us twice. Let's go, Christopher. We'll catch up with you guys in a couple of hours," Marty said heading off with Christopher in tow.

Nearly jogging, Marty whipped out his smartphone. "I've got him. We just follow the red dot."

"What are you talking about?" Christopher asked.

"Wade, who else?" Marty said.

After a few twists and turns, they stumbled upon a scene they couldn't believe. There, in plain sight, behind a large glass-enclosed computer room was Wade dashing between computer servers, manipulating buttons, and staring intently at the lit buttons on a series of portable hard drives, indicating data downloads. He also had a Bluetooth device in his ear and appeared to be communicating with someone.

"What the heck?" Christopher asked.

Marty tried to open the door. No luck. Next, he pulled out his spy kit and went to work. He quickly assembled an array of spy tools on his belt while Christopher did the same. First, he latched on his lock-picking kit. He would need that first. He wasn't sure how Wade had gotten inside, but the door was now locked.

Christopher grabbed a small flashlight off his belt, providing the light Marty needed to work. After a couple of minutes, Marty was able to pull the door open.

He then whipped out his spy camera. He figured if he confronted Wade, one of two things would happen. Wade would either give up, realizing he was outnumbered and that Marty held evidence of his entry, or he would fight. Either way, they needed to be prepared.

Marty held the camera, and quickly threaded his body wire through his shirt and latched it onto his belt buckle. The voice activation feature would come in handy if he could get a confession out of Wade. He also grabbed his stun gun off his spy belt, and patted his trip wire kit.

He hadn't had the heart to try out the stun gun yet, but the Stungun website said the gun delivered enough volts of power to disable a grown man, certainly enough to temporarily subdue. Marty figured one zap would be all he needed. The threat of another zap would hopefully be enough to hold Wade at bay until help arrived.

He motioned to Christopher and they cautiously entered the room. Since they had first spotted him, Wade had continued to dash around from machine to machine like a madman. The teens crept forward. Marty held the spy camera just a few inches from his face.

Suddenly, they pounced. Wade spun around. Marty took the picture, with the recording set on movie, a continuous video was being shot.

"I told you this was none of your business!" Wade shouted.

"You're messing with the Spy Museum," Christopher said. "That makes it our business!"

Marty was reaching for the stun gun as Wade stuck out his hand to grab him. Marty was again reminded that his small frame was no match for the linebacker girth of Wade. He got off a shot that missed its mark.

Behind Wade, Marty could see a set of servers going crazy as their contents appeared to download into the bank of portable hard drives positioned nearby.

Marty and Wade struggled, with Wade eventually using his size to push Marty to the ground and escape from the room.

Marty jumped up, and hesitated a minute to peer at the downloads taking place. The timer showed that numerous megabites had already been transferred. He wondered if he was too late.

"Wait a minute, he's not only downloading data into these portable hard drives. It's being re-directed someplace else. He's getting instructions through his Bluetooth. I've got to go after him!" Marty shouted.

"I'll see what I can do to stop the downloads," Christopher said, plopping down and tackling the first computer.

"Meet up with you later!" Marty called as he ran out after Wade. He shouted over his shoulder. "And watch your back."

Marty's smartphone tracker showed Wade heading back to the group's home base. "Why is he returning?" Marty asked himself aloud. Then, he thought, *what if he's interested in hostages? Sure.*

How else can he get those hard drives out of the museum?

Suddenly, Marty turned and there was Wade, crouched down intently reading the pages of Marty's spy manual. Marty hadn't even realized it was missing. He had no idea that Wade's head now contained an encyclopedia of knowledge. He had studied everything he could get his hands on that covered spy techniques, methodology, and famous spy capers from the past. Now he had finished the last of Marty's coveted spy manual.

Marty thought back to Wade in the tunnel with the two goons. He had wondered what was going on, but had no idea it would have anything to do with his beloved Spy Museum. He worried that somehow this was connected to CRISPR-Cas9.

Marty overheard Wade speak into his Bluetooth. "The download is still in progress. I couldn't stay. They are after me...No, no. I don't know how...Yes, hurry." Wade ended the call and looked all around before running off toward the group base.

Marty took off after him while dialing Christopher.

"Get out of there. He's sending someone to the room to recover the files. He's headed toward base. I've got to get there."

Marty raced off and turned a corner. Wade stood there glaring at him. He grabbed Marty's stun gun and aimed it at the smaller boy. Wade proved to be a better shot than Marty, who fell to his knees in pain. Wade rushed past him with barely a glance.

The pain left as quickly as it had come. Marty hoped that Wade was ignorant of the power of the stun gun. He hoped Wade would think he had more time than he did. *That may be my only advantage,* Marty thought.

As he raised himself up, Granny's words came to mind. "We all think we can do it by ourselves, but it's really the strength of our ancestors that fuels us."

Then he remembered. He had promised his Granny he would not use his powers until she said he could. But what if this does have something to do with CRISPR-Cas9? What if those guys with the drone in the tunnel are using Wade?

Marty took a moment to steel himself and felt stronger. *I can do this,* he thought. *My mission is to save this museum.* He said a prayer that his Granny would understand. "Granny, I think they're trying to bring down the museum. And that's not going to happen, not on my watch," Marty said aloud.

Marty saw Wade sprint down a hall. He pulled out his smartphone and created speed bumps. He pulled out his trip wire kit, and hurled it at Wade's feet. Wade fell, but jumped up immediately. Marty followed him to a door. A glance at his phone tracker revealed the door to be an outer door.

They fell through it, triggering an alarm. As the shrill alarm sounded, Marty and Wade tussled. Wade got loose and took off running. Marty visualized and created a bright, red scooter. Wade dashed in front of him, commandeering the scooter for himself, forcing Marty to generate another one. They zigged and zagged between traffic heading northwest toward the White House.

Marty wasn't sure what Wade and the men he was working for had in mind, but he didn't intend to allow them to unleash their mayhem on the White House. Marty thought of the various concrete barriers surrounding the presidential edifice. He wasn't sure if the place was scooter-proof.

Marty created spinning discs to launch toward Wade's head, thinking that would slow him down enough so Marty could catch him. The only trouble was the effort was slowing Marty down as well. As he retracted the discs and tried to spring his trip wire, Wade veered away from the White House and headed south.

"It's like he's getting directions," Marty said to himself.

In fact, Marty hadn't noticed the tiny earpiece Wade was wearing, a communications piece establishing contact with the goons. Though they seemed to be in total control, the operatives were making it up as they went along, just trying to shake Marty off Wade's trail.

"You must lose him," said Bad Breath.

"Whatever happens, do not let Secret Service capture you. No confessions. We must make it to the private jet. You must leave with us to get what we promised. Now, lose Marty!" Tall Cougher added.

Wade zoomed ahead, nearly colliding with a racing red convertible. He was so focused on eluding Marty, he hardly noticed. Marty sensed time was running out. He created a few nails and spikes in the road. Wade deftly maneuvered around them as if he was on a familiar road course.

Marty stuck with him as Wade headed toward the Potomac River. They raced on, just blocks from the Dr. Martin Luther King, Jr. Memorial. Marty's thoughts flew to his Granny and her description of using her superpowers to help during the U.S. Civil Rights movement. Despite the intensity of the chase, he smiled for a moment. No doubt, his granny had been there during Dr. King's famous "I Have a Dream" speech on the National Mall.

Both scooters raced up to the water's edge. *Whew,* thought Marty. *Somehow I'd rather fight Wade on the water than risk my life in Washington D.C. traffic.*

With motor humming, a boat was waiting. Marty whipped out his phone and created a jet ski. It roared to life as he ran toward it. Wade shot a glance his way. Another jet ski materialized. Marty realized his focus was off.

Wade ran toward the watercraft and jumped on, thinking he could lose Marty more quickly and could double-back and get on the boat later. Marty jumped on the second jet ski and the chase was on. A dark, bearded man was on board the boat waiting for Wade. He saw what was happening and shouted into his smartphone.

Marty was too far away to hear what he said. The noise from their machines blocked out any other sound. Wade zipped in front of Marty, sending up a spray of water. Marty zigged and zagged from side to side to avoid some of the shooting water while still keeping Wade in his sights.

The boys sped down the Potomac, nearing a golf course. Marty whipped out his smartphone and steered the bobbing watercraft with one hand.

I have to stop him fast before he either crashes without telling us what he was up to and who he's working with, or he gets away, Marty thought.

Marty created a row of floating barriers. Wade deftly navigated away from the obstructions and continued on his way.

Next, Marty sent out an array of flapping, shrieking seagulls that behaved as if Wade were one large morsel. They alternately dived at Wade, pecking at him and blocking his view. He ducked and dodged. The seagulls kept coming. Still, Wade was able to maneuver closer to the shoreline than Marty thought.

Suddenly, Wade's jet ski struck land. Wade jumped off and took off running. Marty followed suit, beached his watercraft, and ran after Wade, who fumbled for the bag he wore slung over his shoulder.

Marty swallowed the lump in his throat, and managed to leave a message. "Christopher, it's me. I'm still in pursuit. He's handling everything I'm throwing at him. I'm trying to figure out what's going on. I saw at least one of his accomplices. So stay put. Alert the museum security staff. I'll get back in touch when I..."

Before Marty could finish the sentence, a blinding light flashed at him. He had heard of the Titanic light machine, but had never actually experienced it. He felt as if he were in the tumultuous waters of the Atlantic Ocean. His stomach began to roll and he felt sicker than he could ever remember.

Wade laughed as he again aimed his weapon at Marty. He then took off running. Marty slowly pulled himself upright, as he watched Wade getting away. *I can't let that happen,* he thought as he willed himself to take off after Wade.

He quickly pulled himself together and produced his fleet of soldiers. He touched the Order of Hannibal medal stored securely in his jacket pocket. The four-foot tall soldiers seemed to have superfueled their diets.

"Oh, yeah, they're not real," he said under his breath. Once again, Marty could have sworn he saw chests rising up and down with the effort of breathing. These soldiers must have been at least seven feet tall! With the medal, everything appeared to be magnified, and it was.

28
CHRISTOPHER SEEKS
OUT SECURITY

Christopher rushed back to home base looking for the group leader. Ian was nowhere to be found. Instead, Christopher stumbled upon a security guard. He found him examining a new spy exhibit.

"I need to talk to you," Christopher yelled, running up to the guard.

"Whoa, little buddy. What's up?" the security guard asked.

"It's my friend. He's in real trouble. I'm in contact via communications. He ran outside chasing Wade, the bully, and now they're racing through the streets. We need to call the D.C. police," Christopher said, breathlessly.

"Wait, your friend was here for the spy overnight? He can't leave the building. That's a serious breach. I'm going to have to call this in," he said reaching for his walkie-talkie.

Christopher led the security guard and his supervisor to the area where the museum's computers were housed. The supervisor's gap jawed surprise at the disarray of portable hard drives, clearly abandoned, spoke volumes. He immediately called the F.B.I.

The agent on the other end of the line was incredulous. "How could they possibly learn the access code?" he asked.

"I don't know, Agent Lee, but it's clear that whoever got in here knew what they were doing. Let's hope they panicked and abandoned it before they downloaded the data. From the looks of it, that's exactly what happened."

* * * * *

Remotely, the goons who hired Wade were chuckling among themselves.

"Damn, you were right. That kid was the right choice. His idea to include the portable hard drives as a distraction should give us the space we need to get out of town. We've got everything we need," Bad Breath said.

Tall Cougher laughed, then coughed harshly, and slapped the shorter man on the back. "Yeah, and he can find his own way out of town."

"Can't we at least stay to see his face when he realizes he's not getting a thing for this caper? We walk away with data worth millions, maybe even billions, and he gets…jail time, if he's lucky."

"Our orders are to eradicate the trail. The kid included."

Tall Cougher's chest rose and fell with his continuous coughing fit. They were preparing to abandon a kid who had helped with the caper of the century. That is, once he was made aware of his innate ability to memorize vast quantities of data in minutes, and he did so skillfully. He didn't even ask questions about what the data contained.

29
MARTY DEPUTIZES WADE

Wade rolled into what must have been a sand bunker on hole 13 of the golf course. His chest heaved as he sought to catch his breath. Wade activated the audio to the tracker. He had learned from the spy manual that any good spy stays one step ahead of the bad guys. As he listened in on the conversation the goons were having, he sobbed.

"They duped me! No more missions, no more defeating guys who think they're smarter than me?" Wade yelled, blubbering all the while.

He sobbed into his sleeve. Marty listened.

"That's the one thing. The one thing I needed! No one asks me to sit at their stupid lunch table or go to their stupid parties."

Marty stopped in his tracks.

He had lost track of Wade for a few minutes and was tweaking his tracker to better locate his classmate when he heard the scream. It sounded unreal, like the cry of a trapped, wounded animal. Marty's hair stood up on the back of his neck. *It must be a trick of some kind,* he thought.

He wildly looked around the vast golf course. *I wonder if Wade has a sophisticated voice changer.* Marty knew walking out in plain sight to investigate could be a formula for disaster.

Then the sound came again. *Wait! Is Wade crying? Did they really trick him?* Marty couldn't help himself. He followed the sound to the side of the bunker, where he found Wade sobbing. Marty stood over him, dumbfounded. Wade glanced up once or twice but didn't try to cover his face or run away. Marty just stood there until the cries dissolved into moans.

Instead of seeing a devious spy, Marty now saw a scared little boy.

"What's up?" he asked, keeping one hand on his spy belt just in case.

"I'm not gonna…They never planned…" was all Wade said before dissolving into tears again. He kicked at the sand surrounding him.

Marty jumped into the sand bunker and sat down next to Wade. He awkwardly extended his hand, and touched Wade on the shoulder.

"It's over!" Wade screamed. "They duped me!"

"Who?"

"My so-called partners. They never intended to share anything with me. This was...all for nothing," Wade moaned.

Marty couldn't believe what he was hearing. The mission was over? Then he remembered the downloaded data.

"That's where you're wrong, Wade. It isn't over. What a sniveling idiot you are! Don't you realize the damage is already done? You've already given up the data. They couldn't have done it without you. So you're an accessory. Whether you want to admit that or not," Marty said.

Wade began to blubber again. They sat that way for a while. Wade in tears. And Marty in deep thought.

Then, Marty had an idea. "Hey, tell me everything you know about your mission."

When Wade finished talking, it was nearly pitch dark on the golf course. Marty turned on his smartphone flashlight, reached into a small jar hooked onto his spy belt, pulled out black eye cream and smeared it below his eyes, then nodded to Wade who leaned over, and Marty applied the cream to Wade.

"You've been deputized. Now here's what we're going to do..." Marty said.

* * * * *

Marty and Wade slowly crept up to the clubhouse where the goon team had assembled. The front door stood wide open. The two guys Wade had worked for had been joined by two comrades. They were giddy with their victory and totally unaware of the kids.

Marty closed his eyes and touched his medal. Wade shuddered when he saw Marty's band of soldiers materializing.

Now the dozen soldiers were about seven feet tall and cloaked in metal armor. Each soldier held a bayonet along with a high-tech device Wade didn't recognize. Their slitted eyes gave the appearance of a 21st-century extra-terrestrial. As if awaiting a command from their commander-in-chief, Marty Hayes, they stood at rapt attention.

One of the goons finally noticed, and with eyes wide, motioned to his nearest co-conspirator. Smiles changed to stunned frowns.

Marty gave an invisible command. Wade could only guess at what happened. He breathed a sigh of relief now that he was part of Marty's team. The goons who had appeared so powerful since the moment they met, were now struck with fear. One reached for a weapon. A soldier promptly zapped it out of his hand.

His eyes mirrored his disbelief. Marty saw the tall, coughing man reach toward his hip.

"He's going for a weapon!" Wade yelled.

Marty quickly gave a nod to the nearest soldier. The soldier flicked the item out of reach.

"We have to get out of here," Marty said.

He headed toward the open door, pushing a soldier ahead of him. He closed his eyes, materializing a large jail cell.

"Wade, you go with them," Marty ordered. "Take the scum to the jail cell and contain them while I have a little chat with these two." He nodded toward Tall Cougher and Bad Breath.

Marty's sweaty palm touched the phone. The soldier disappeared.

"What the…?" Marty gasped.

He had mistakenly provided the opening the goons needed. Tall Cougher advanced on Marty. He was close enough that Marty could smell his breath. The smaller man joined the party, with Marty thinking he was going to collapse just from the fumes of his bad breath.

"So your reinforcements are gone. Now what do you think you're going to do, Mr. Marty, smart guy?" he asked.

Marty took a step back.

"Don't even think about it. Hand over that phone," Tall Cougher ordered.

Before Marty could react, the goon snatched the phone out of Marty's hand, leaving the boy defenseless.

"What's our plan?" the goon then asked his comrades.

30

KIDS OF WINDSOR MIDDLE SCHOOL: READY FOR ACTION!

Christopher paced the museum floor. He turned to the security guy. "What's going on? Shouldn't we have heard something by now?" he asked.

"Keep your shoes on, kid. We've alerted the F.B.I. and Secret Service. They're on it," the security guy answered.

"F.B.I. and Secret Service?" Christopher asked. "I thought you were the guys going after Marty. Why? Why are they even involved?"

He gave Christopher a long look. "Johnny, take the kid to the cafeteria and get him whatever he wants. Keep him busy. We'll contact you both when we have something to report."

"Got you," Johnny said, moving closer to Christopher.

"Hold on! I've got valuable information you may need to crack this case. I'm not leaving!" Christopher said.

"We didn't ask for your help, kid. Go with Johnny here and we'll keep you posted," the lead security guy said.

Christopher noted Johnny's bulk. He shrugged and headed toward the door. Just as his foot was about to cross the doorframe, Christopher made a lurch forward and began running as fast as he had ever run. Security Officer Johnny was caught off guard. In the seconds it took for him to realize what was happening, Christopher was shooting down the hall, his arms and legs furiously pumping.

It didn't take long for Christopher to lose the officer, who had to slow down. Christopher ducked around a corner and bent over to catch his breath.

"I was wondering when you were going to come back to find me," a familiar voice said.

Christopher jumped, and turned to face Aisha. There was something different about her. She was fully suited up in her usual bright purple, but around her waist was an array of gadgets.

Christopher's eyes widened. "Oh, my gosh! You've got to be kidding me. What are you doing here?"

"I'll explain later. Right now, we need to find out why Marty hasn't responded."

Christopher gave her a look.

"Yes, I know about Wade. And I'm equipped to help," Aisha said, revealing a belt with spy gadgets attached.

"You're equipped to help," Christopher repeated, sizing up her gadgetry. "Come on, I'll brief you on the way." He headed for the same door Marty and Wade had exited.

Christopher pulled out his tracker. "They're on the banks of the Potomac, looks like there's some sort of golf course nearby. That's just a few miles away from here."

"We've got to get to them," Aisha said, hurrying along. They opened the door, setting off the squealing alarm. As the security team reacted, Aisha and Christopher made their exit. They raced toward the metro station, easily fading into the night.

Once they settled into their seats on the train, Christopher turned to Aisha.

"If only we had daylight in our favor. I didn't think to bring my night vision goggles," Christopher said quietly, taking care not to be overheard by their fellow passengers.

"Trust me. We won't need them," Aisha said.

"Oh, I guess you can see in the dark," Christopher said, sarcastically.

"Actually, I can," Aisha said.

Christopher jumped. "Just what are you saying?"

Aisha took a deep breath. "I know Marty has shared information about his powers with you. Well, I have … I have night vision. I mean … without any need for goggles or lenses."

"Are you kidding me?" Christopher threw his hands up to his face. "What is this? Why am I the only one who seems to have taken the normal kid pill and everyone else get the superpowers?"

Aisha laughed. "Maybe yours haven't been revealed to you."

Christopher grinned. "Really?"

"Ok, so I'm just trying to make you feel better. But for now, let's find Marty. He needs our help. If you've been working with gadgets as long as Marty has, you can help. Let's go."

Minutes later, Aisha and Christopher crept up to the clubhouse. The door was closed. He double-checked. Yes, the tracker clearly indicated that Marty was inside. Now that they had located him, Christopher felt his steady drumbeat of adrenaline deflate, replaced by fear.

Compounding things was the stark darkness that surrounded them. They didn't know what Marty was facing inside. Then Christopher remembered Aisha's special powers. He hoped she knew how to use them to her advantage.

Inside the clubhouse, Marty sat silently. His phone and jacket had been thrown to one side. His medal was in his jacket pocket. And worse, he was tied up with rope! His heart was beating so fast that he couldn't even think of imagining a creation and he certainly couldn't control anything without his medal. He wondered what Christopher was doing. He was sure his buddy would be very worried about him and working hard to find him.

Darn it! He cursed himself. *What if Christopher can't get me out of this fix without hurting himself? I couldn't live with myself if I let him down. It was my idea to go after Wade. I didn't really know what we were dealing with.*

Marty felt tears spring to his eyes. Then, he heard his granny's voice in his head and felt her presence.

He thought, *I'm a Hayes and we're no quitters.* If Granny took on the bigots of the Civil Rights era, surely I can survive this. Marty's head cocked to one side. He had heard something outside.

Tall Cougher slowly opened the door and stepped outside to investigate. Out of view of those remaining inside, Aisha had taken advantage of the darkness that inhibited everyone there but her, and tripped up the goon. As he lay on the ground, wildly looking around for who had knocked him down, Aisha grabbed duct tape off her spy belt, muffled him, and pushed him off to the side. She then nodded to Christopher to repeat the noises to draw out the goons.

Bad Breath went outside, this time to find out the source of the knocking. As he walked out into the darkness, Aisha and Christopher worked together using their trip wire, and unleashed their trick lasso to capture the goon.

"It's a bunch of kids. Subdue Marty!" he yelled.

Upon hearing that, Marty's pulse quickened. He grabbed his jacket and quickly located his medal and smartphone. Marty raced outside and blinked with surprise at the sight of Christopher and Aisha. Standing above the goon was Wade. The Titanic gun came in handy.

Wade looked around him. Marty was pretty certain he was looking for the other goon who had first recruited him. Wade trained his Titanic on him. Marty successfully reached them both and handcuffed them to the nearest tree. He winked at Wade.

"Glad to see you, buddy," he said.

Wade nodded. His chest filled with pride.

"Secret Service! We'll take it from here," an adult voice shouted.

Christopher, Aisha, and Marty huddled together in relief and satisfaction at the successful conclusion of their caper. Marty caught Aisha's eye. They stared at each other for a long moment.

31
CELEBRATION DAY FOR WINDSOR MIDDLE SCHOOL'S HEROES AND SHEROES

Wheels up! The plane lifted up from Reagan National airport.

The F.B.I. agent who interviewed Marty wouldn't say for sure what type of data the goons were after. But, when Marty asked if it had anything to do with CRISPR-Cas9, the agent's response, "I can neither confirm nor deny," had told Marty all he needed to know. He had long suspected the ground-breaking science with its ability to make billions would attract the unscrupulous along with those who wanted to eradicate diseases.

Wade, Christopher, and Mrs. Hayes sat in one row. Just ahead of them were Aisha and Marty. Mrs. Hayes threw them a look as Marty's friends pointed and giggled. She hadn't heard much about this

Wade, but with his abilities, she was pretty certain he came from the Order of Hannibal lineage.

"What I really want to know is how you were able to convince your parents to allow you to come to Washington, D.C. on your own," Marty asked Aisha.

Aisha shrugged. "That's a lo-o-n-g story for another time." She ran her fingers along her medal. "So I hear your granny is also in the Old Ladies' Aerobic Club."

"Senior Ladies," Marty corrected. "What? Your granny, too?"

"Shhh…" Aisha put a finger to her lips. "Do you think only boys get the powers?"

* * * * *

The restless middle schoolers at Windsor danced in their seats waiting for someone to take the stage. A procession began. First out was Principal Smiley, followed by Marty, Christopher, Aisha, and Wade. Nervous chattering sounded.

"What the heck is the school bully doing on stage?" one kid loudly asked.

The group took their seats. Mr. Bunsen, next on stage, headed immediately to the microphone.

"Good morning, students. We're assembling here today to honor a few of our own," he said.

"It's a science award," the kid said, nudging his neighbor.

"If you're thinking we're here for a science award, you're mistaken," said Mr. Bunsen.

The nudged student eyed his fellow student. "Got another guess?"

"So, let me tell you why we're here. Thanks to the heroic efforts of four of our own Windsor students, the Secret Service was able to get enough evidence on the Moisov gang to send them away for a while."

Marty, Christopher, Aisha, and Wade shared a knowing smile.

Marty noticed that Aisha unconsciously touched her hand to her heart where her medal lay. Granny also noticed and leaned into the friend by her side.

"It wasn't just my grandchild's time to come into his powers. Your grandbaby was the final piece to solve that puzzle," she said.

Janet smiled knowingly. "I had the talk with her right around the time you told me about Marty. You were so concerned about him that I didn't want to tell you about her right then."

Granny patted her hand. "The next generation has it handled. I'm sure you're as proud as I am."

Janet nodded and hugged her friend. Granny's eyes drifted over to Toni, who for a change, was sitting still with a firm grip on her lion king. Granny had to close her eyes for a second. She could have sworn she saw the lion king move. Not my granddaughter, too, she thought. Granny sighed deeply.

"Toni, come here and sit by me, baby. We need to have a little talk."

Mr. Smiley cleared his throat. "So please join me in congratulating Marty Hayes, Christopher Greene, Aisha Harris, and Wade Crumbly. The U.S. government has awarded us with $10,000 to go towards our CRISPR-Cas9 research. In addition, the four students will each receive a $1,000 gift card for the International Spy Museum and lifetime membership.

Marty beamed and began to high five his friends on stage. He ended with a jumping high five for Principal Smiley.

THE END

ACKNOWLEDGMENTS

I owe a debt of gratitude to the village that helped bring *The Stupendous Adventures of Mighty Marty Hayes* to life. I appreciate everyone who provided encouragement throughout my journey toward publication.

Thank you, family and friends.

Special recognition goes to my son, William Pinckney, who served as the initial inspiration for Mighty Marty, along with my rock and husband, No. 1 Supporter-in-Chief, Kenneth Pinckney. Many thanks to Mary Pinckney, the best mother-in-law ever!

Thanks also goes to near lifelong friends, who never wavered in their support, Patricia Dunn, Patricia Waddell and Joyce Taylor. And yes, to my dear neighbor, Lori Talasek, who always wanted to know, "Is the book finished?" Lori, it's done.

This small-town Wisconsin girl lived vicariously through Pippi Longstocking, and developed as an adult through the written treasures of Maya Angelou and Khalil Gibran.

I salute every English teacher, librarian, bookstore and coffee shop owner who has nurtured far more authors than they will ever know.

I salute everyone working in publishing who join me in my mission to ensure children of all colors, and unique characteristics, find themselves reflected in the pages of a book.

I owe it all to my parents, Haward and Leona Hyler. It all began with sets of children bible stories, read at bedtime.

And finally, I appreciate all the drivers in Racine, Wis., who swerved around the little girl as she stepped haphazardly into traffic, walking to and from school with her nose buried in the pages of a book. That was me.

ABOUT THE AUTHOR

Lora Hyler carried her love of reading and writing into a radio news career as a reporter for NPR affiliate, WUWM and ABC affiliate, WISN, both in Milwaukee, Wis. She also had a corporate career in writing, editing and strategic communications management. She started her public relations and marketing company, Hyler Communications, in 2001.

Lora has written hundreds of articles, several screenplays, short stories, and a novel. *The Stupendous Adventures of Mighty Marty Hayes* is the first in a three-part series. The second novel, planned for 2019, features Aisha, who further uses her night vision powers to save the day. Girl power!

Lora holds a 2016 Jade Ring award from the Wisconsin Writers Association (WWA), along with several screenwriting and news awards.

Her sense of adventure began as she discovered childhood favorites, Pippi Longstocking and Charlie and the Chocolate Factory. Her adventure-writing often began with real life travel adventures to children museums and distant lands.

She has twice been awarded a writer's residency at Noepe Center for the Literary Arts on Martha's Vineyard, Mass. (2015 & 2016), and was selected for a May 2017 month-long artist residency in Marnay-sur-Seine, France. She'll return for another residency in February 2019 in Cassis, in the south of France.

More about Lora at
www.hylercommunications.com/creative

CPSIA information can be obtained
at www.ICGtesting.com
Printed in the USA
BVHW04s1531191018
530658BV00003B/11/P